"Sorry, Bree," Vladimir tossed his card on the table.

Bree stared down at the king of diamonds.

Her mind went blank. Then a tremble went through her, starting at her toes and shaking up her body as she looked up at Vladimir, her eyes wide and uncomprehending. "You…you've…" Bree couldn't speak the words.

"I've won." Vladimir looked at her, his blue eyes electric with dislike. He rose from his chair, all six feet four inches of him, and said coldly, "You have ten minutes to pack. I will collect my winnings in the lobby." As she gaped up at him, he walked around the table to stand over her, so close she could feel the warmth of his body. He leaned over, his face inches from hers.

"I've waited a long time for this," he said softly. "But now, at last, Bree Dalton—" his lips slid into a hard, sensual smile *"—you are mine."*

PRINCES
Untamed

Only the most innocent touch can melt their ice-cold hearts

Introducing the notoriously ruthless and devilishly sexy Princes Kasimir and Vladimir Xendzov: two brothers torn apart by the past, bitter rivals in the present.

DEALING HER FINAL CARD

February 2013

Vladimir's enemy is most definitely in his sight—he can't take his eyes off her! But she's played her final card…and he knows he's going to win.

Look out for...

A REPUTATION FOR REVENGE

Coming in March 2013

Kasimir will consume everything in his path on his road to revenge…even if the obstacle standing in his way is five feet five inches of pure desire.

Jennie Lucas

DEALING HER FINAL CARD

PRINCES
Untamed

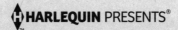
HARLEQUIN PRESENTS®

If you purchased this book without a cover you should be aware that this book is stolen property. It was reported as "unsold and destroyed" to the publisher, and neither the author nor the publisher has received any payment for this "stripped book."

Recycling programs
for this product may
not exist in your area.

ISBN-13: 978-0-373-13122-8

DEALING HER FINAL CARD

Copyright © 2013 by Jennie Lucas

All rights reserved. Except for use in any review, the reproduction or utilization of this work in whole or in part in any form by any electronic, mechanical or other means, now known or hereafter invented, including xerography, photocopying and recording, or in any information storage or retrieval system, is forbidden without the written permission of the publisher, Harlequin Enterprises Limited, 225 Duncan Mill Road, Don Mills, Ontario M3B 3K9, Canada.

This is a work of fiction. Names, characters, places and incidents are either the product of the author's imagination or are used fictitiously, and any resemblance to actual persons, living or dead, business establishments, events or locales is entirely coincidental.

This edition published by arrangement with Harlequin Books S.A.

For questions and comments about the quality of this book, please contact us at CustomerService@Harlequin.com.

® and TM are trademarks of Harlequin Enterprises Limited or its corporate affiliates. Trademarks indicated with ® are registered in the United States Patent and Trademark Office, the Canadian Trade Marks Office and in other countries.

Printed in U.S.A.

All about the author…
Jennie Lucas

JENNIE LUCAS had a tragic beginning for any would-be writer: a very happy childhood. Her parents owned a bookstore, and she grew up surrounded by books, dreaming about faraway lands. When she was ten, her father secretly paid her a dollar for every classic novel *(Jane Eyre, War and Peace)* that she read.

At fifteen, she went to a Connecticut boarding school on scholarship. She took her first solo trip to Europe at sixteen, then put off college and traveled around the United States, supporting herself with jobs as diverse as gas station cashier and newspaper advertising assistant.

At 22, she met the man who would become her husband. For the first time in her life, she wanted to stay in one place, as long as she could be with him. After their marriage, she graduated from Kent State University with a degree in English, and started writing books a year later.

Jennie was a finalist in the Romance Writers of America's Golden Heart contest in 2003 and won the award in 2005. A fellow 2003 finalist, Australian author Trish Morey, read Jennie's writing and told her that she should write for Harlequin® Presents. It seemed like too big a dream, but Jennie took a deep breath and went for it. A year later Jennie got the magical call from London that turned her into a published author.

Since then, life has been hectic, juggling a writing career, a sexy husband and two young children, but Jennie loves her crazy, chaotic life. Now if she can only figure out how to pack up her family and live in all the places she's writing about!

For more about Jennie and her books, please visit her website at www.jennielucas.com.

Other titles by Jennie Lucas available in ebook:

Harlequin Presents®

CHAPTER ONE

"BREE, wake up!"

A hand roughly shook Bree Dalton awake. Startled, she sat up with a gasp, blinking in the darkness.

Her younger sister was sitting on the edge of the bed. Tears sparkled on Josie's pale cheeks in the moonlight.

"What's happened?" Bree dropped her bare feet to the tile floor, ready to run, ready to fight anyone who had made her baby sister cry. "What's wrong?"

Josie took a deep breath.

"I really messed up this time." She wiped her eyes. "But before you freak out, I want you to know it's going to be fine. I know how to fix it."

Rather than be comforted by this statement, Bree felt deepening fear. Her twenty-two-year-old sister, six years younger than Bree, had a knack for getting into trouble. And she was wearing the short, sexy dress of a Hale Ka'nani cocktail waitress instead of their gray housekeeping smock.

"Were you working at the bar?" Bree demanded.

"Still worried about some man hitting on me?" Josie barked a bitter laugh. "I *wish* that was the problem."

"What is it, then?"

Josie ran a hand over her eyes. "I'm tired, Bree," she whispered. "You gave up everything to take care of me. When I was twelve, I needed that, but now I am so tired of being your burden—"

"I've never thought of you that way," Bree said, stung.

Josie looked at her clasped hands. "I thought this was my chance to pay off those debts, so we could go back to the Mainland. I've been practicing in secret. I thought I knew how to play. How to win."

A chill went down Bree's spine.

"You gambled?" she said numbly.

"It fell into my lap." Josie exhaled, visibly shivering in the warm Hawaiian night. "I'd finished cleaning the wedding reception in the ballroom when I ran into Mr. Hudson. He offered to pay me overtime if I'd serve drinks at his private poker game at midnight. I knew you'd say no, but I thought, just this once…"

"I told you not to trust him!"

"I'm sorry," Josie cried. "When he invited me to join them at the table, I couldn't say no!"

Bree clawed back her long blond hair. "What happened?"

"I won," Josie said defiantly. Then she swallowed. "At least I did for a while. Then I started losing. First I lost the chips I'd won, then I lost our grocery money, and then…"

Cold understanding went through Bree. She finished dully, "Then Mr. Hudson kindly offered to loan you whatever you needed."

Josie's mouth fell open. "How did you know?"

Because Bree knew bullies like Greg Hudson and how they tried to gain the upper hand. She'd met his type before, long ago, in the life she'd given up ten years ago—before she'd fallen in love, and her life had fallen apart. Before the man she loved had betrayed her, leaving her to the sheriff and the wolves—orphaned and penniless at eighteen, with a heartbroken twelve-year-old sister.

But oh, yes. Bree knew Greg Hudson's type. She closed her eyes, feeling sick as she thought of the hotel manager's hard eyes above his jovial smile, of his cheerful Hawaiian shirt that barely covered his fat belly. The resort manager had slept with many of his female employees, particularly amongst the lower-paid housekeeping staff. In the two months since the Dalton sisters had arrived in Hawaii, Bree had wondered more than once why he'd gone to such trouble to hire them from Seattle. He claimed the girls had been recommended by their employment agency, but that didn't ring true. Surely there were many people looking for jobs here in Honolulu.

Josie had laughed at her, teasing her for being "gloomy and doomy," but as Bree had scrubbed the bathrooms and floors of the lavish resort, she'd tried to solve the puzzle in her mind, and her bad feeling only grew. Especially when their boss made it clear over the past few weeks that he was interested in Josie. And made it equally clear the one he really wanted was Bree.

But of course Josie, with her innocent, trusting spirit, never noticed evil around her. She didn't fully understand why Bree had given up gambling, and insisted they work only low-wage jobs for the ten years since their father died, keeping them under the radar of unscrupulous, dangerous men. Josie didn't know how wicked the world could be.

Bree did.

"Gambling doesn't pay." She kept her voice calm. "You should know that by now."

"You're wrong. It does!" Josie said angrily. "We had plenty of money ten years ago." She turned and looked wistfully at the window, toward the moonlit Hawaiian night. "And I thought if I could just be more like you and Dad…"

"You were using *us* as role models? Have you lost your mind?" Bree exploded. "I've spent the last decade trying to give you a different life!"

"Don't you think I know that?" Josie cried. "What you've sacrificed for me?"

Bree took a deep breath. "It wasn't just for you." Her throat ached as she rose to her feet. "How much money did you lose tonight?"

For a moment, her sister didn't answer. Outside, Bree heard

the distant plaintive call of seabirds as Josie stared mutinously at the floor, arms folded. When she finally spoke, her voice was barely audible.

"A hundred."

Bree felt relief so fierce she almost cried. She'd been so afraid it would be worse. Reaching out, she gave her sister's shoulder a squeeze. "It'll be all right." She exhaled in relief. "Our budget will be tight, but we'll just eat a little more rice and beans this month." Wiping her eyes, she tried to smile. "Let this be a good lesson…"

But Josie hadn't moved from the end of the bed. She looked up, her face pale.

"A hundred *thousand,* Bree," she whispered. "I owe Mr. Hudson a hundred thousand dollars."

For a second, Bree couldn't understand the words. Lingering tears of relief burned her eyes like acid as she stared at her sister.

A hundred thousand dollars.

Turning away, Bree started to pace, compulsively twisting a long tendril of blond hair into a tight ringlet around her finger as she struggled to make sense of all her worst fears coming true. She tried to control her shaking hands. Tried desperately to think of a way out.

"But I told you, you don't have to worry!" Josie blurted out. "I have a plan."

Bree stopped abruptly. "What is it?"

"I'm going to sell the land."

Her eyes went wide as she stared at her sister.

"There's no choice now. Even you must see that," Josie argued, blinking fast as she clasped her hands tightly in her lap. "We'll sell it, pay off the debt, and then pay off those men who are after us. You'll finally be free—"

"That land is in trust." Bree's voice was hard. "You don't get possession until you're twenty-five or married. So put it out of your mind."

Josie shook her head desperately. "But I know how I could—"

"You can't," she said coldly. "And even if you could, I wouldn't let you. Dad put that land into an unbreakable trust for a reason."

"Because he thought I was helpless to take care of myself."

"Because from the day you were born, you've had a knack for trusting people and believing the best of them."

"You mean I'm stupid and naive."

Controlling herself, Bree clenched her hands at her sides.

"It's a good quality, Josie," she said quietly. "I wish I had more of it."

And it was true. Josie had always put concern for others over her own safety and well-being. As a chubby girl of five, she'd once wandered out of their Alaskan cabin into the snow, hoping to find their neighbor's cat, which had disappeared the day before. Eleven-year-old Bree had searched their rural street with their panicked father and half a dozen neighbors for hours, until they'd finally found her, lost in the forest, dazed and half-frozen.

Josie had nearly died that day, for the sake of a cat that was found later, snug and warm in a nearby barn.

Bree took a deep breath. Her little sister's heart was as big as the world. It was why she needed someone not nearly so kind or innocent to protect her. "Are they still playing?"

"Yes," Josie said in a small voice.

"Who's at the table?"

"Mr. Hudson and a few owners. Texas Big-Hat, Silicon Valley, Belgian Bob," she said, using the housekeeping staff's nicknames for the villa owners. Her eyes narrowed. "And one more man I didn't recognize. Handsome. Arrogant. He kicked me out of the game." She scowled. "The others would've let me stay longer—"

"You would have just lost more," Bree said coldly. Turning away, she went behind her closet door and yanked off her oversized sleep shirt, pulling on a bra and then a snug black T-shirt. "We'd owe a million dollars now, instead of just a hundred thousand."

"It might as well be a million, for all our chance of paying," Josie grumbled. "For all the good it will do them if I don't sell that land. They can't get blood out of a stone!"

Bree pulled on her skinny dark jeans over her slim legs. "And what do you think will happen when you don't pay?"

"Mr. Hudson will make me scrub his floors for free?" she replied weakly.

Coming around the closet door, Bree stared at her in disbelief. "Scrub his *floors?*"

"What else can he do?"

Bree turned away, muttering to herself. Josie didn't understand the situation she was dealing with. How could she? Bree had made it her mission in life to protect her from knowing.

She'd hoped they would find peace in Hawaii, three thousand miles away from the ice and snow of Alaska. She'd prayed she would find her own peace, and finally stop dreaming of the blue-eyed, dark-haired man she'd once loved. But it hadn't worked. Every night, she still felt Vladimir's arms around her, still heard his low, sensual voice. *I love you, Breanna.* She still saw the brightness of his eyes as he held up a sparkling diamond beneath the Christmas tree. *Will you marry me?*

Ugh. Furiously, Bree pushed the memory away. No wonder she still hated Christmas. Let other women go home to their turkeys and children and brightly lit trees. To Bree, yesterday had been just another workday. She never let herself remember that one magical Christmas night when she was eighteen, when she'd wanted to change her life to be worthy of Vladimir's love. The night she'd promised herself that she would never—for any reason—gamble or cheat or lie again. Even though he'd left her, she'd kept that promise.

Until now. She reached into the back of her closet, pulling out her black boots with the sharp stiletto heels.

"Bree?" Josie said anxiously.

Not answering, Bree sat down heavily on the bed. Putting her feet into her boots, she zipped up the backs. It was the first time she'd worn these stiletto boots since she was a rebellious teenager with a flexible conscience and a greedy heart. It took Bree back to the woman she'd never thought she would be again. The woman she'd have to be tonight to save her sister. She glanced at the illuminated red letters of the clock. Three in the morning. A perfect time to start.

"Please, you don't have to do this," her sister whimpered. Her voice choked as she whispered helplessly, "I have a plan."

Ignoring the guilt and anguish in her sister's voice, Bree rose to her feet. "Stay here." Squaring her shoulders, she severed the connection between her brain and her pounding heart. Emotion would only be a liability from here on out. "I'll take care of it."

"No! It's my fault, Bree, and I can fix it. Listen. On Christmas Eve, I met a man who told me how…"

But Bree didn't wait to hear whatever cockamamy sob story someone might have fed her softhearted sister this time. She grabbed her black leather motorcycle jacket and headed for the door.

"Bree, wait!"

She didn't look back. She walked out of the tiny apartment and went down the open-air hallway to the moss-covered, crumbling concrete steps of the aging building where all the Hale Ka'nani Resort's staff lived.

It's just like riding a bike, Bree told herself fiercely as she raced down the steps. Even after ten years away from the game, she could win at poker. She *could.*

Warm trade winds blew against her cold skin. Pulling on her black leather jacket, she went down the illuminated paths of the five-star resort toward the beautiful, brand-new buildings used by wealthy tourists and the even wealthier villa owners, clustered around the edge of a private, white-sand beach.

My heart is cold, she repeated to herself. *I feel nothing.*

The moon was full over the Pacific, leaving a ghostly trail across the black water. Palm trees swayed in the warmth of the Hawaiian breeze. She heard the distant call of night birds, smelled the exotic scent of fruit and spice mingling with the salt of the sea.

Above her, dark silhouettes of tall, slender palm trees swayed in a violet sky twinkling with stars. Even with the bright full moon, the night seemed black to her, wide and endless as the sea. She followed the illuminated path around the deserted pool between the beach and the main lobby. As she grew closer to the beach, she heard the sound of the surf build to a roar.

The open-air bar was nearly empty beneath its long thatched roof. Hanging lights swayed in the breeze over a few drunk tourists and cuddling honeymooners. Bree nodded at the tired-eyed bartender, then went past the bar into a connecting hall that led to the private rooms reserved for the villa owners and their guests. Where rich men brought their cheap mistresses and played private, illegal games.

Opening the door, Bree stumbled in her stiletto boots.

Clenching her hands at her sides, she took a deep breath and told her heart to be a lump of ice. Cold. Cold. Cold. She had no feelings of any kind. Poker was easy. By the time she was fourteen, she'd been fleecing tourists in Alaskan ports. And she'd learned the best way not to show emotion was not to feel it in the first place.

Never play with your heart, kiddo. Only a sucker plays with his heart. Even if you win, you lose.

Her father had said those words to her a million times growing up, but she'd still had to learn the hard way. Once, she'd played with all her heart. And lost—everything.

Don't think about it. But in spite of her best efforts, the memory brought a chill of fear. She'd been so determined to leave that life behind. What if she'd forgotten how to play? What if she'd lost her gift? What if she couldn't lure the men in, convince them to let her ante up without money, and get the cards she needed—or bluff them into believing she had?

If she failed at this, then… Bree felt a flash of sweat on her forehead. Running for the Mainland might be their only option. Or, since they had no money or credit cards and it was doubtful they'd even make it to the airport before they were caught, *swimming* for the Mainland.

She exhaled, forcing her body to calm down and her heart to slow. *It's just poker,* she told herself firmly. *Your heart is cold. You feel nothing.*

Bree went all the way down the long, air-conditioned hall. A large man weighing perhaps three hundred pounds sat at a polished oak door.

She forced a crooked smile in his direction. "Hey, Kai."

The enormous security guard nodded with a single jerk of his chins. "What you doing here, Bree? Saw your sister take off. She sick or something?"

"Something like that."

"You working in her place?" Kai frowned, looking over her dark, tight jeans, her black leather jacket and black stiletto boots. "Where's the uniform?"

"This is my outfit." Her voice was cool as she stared him down. "For poker."

"Oh." His round, friendly face looked confused. "Well. Okay. Go in, then."

"Thanks." Forcing the ice in her voice to fully infuse her heart, she pushed open the door.

The private room for the villa residents had a cavernous ceiling and no windows. The walls were soundproofed with thick red fabric that swooped from a center point on the ceiling. The effect made the room glamorous and cozy and claustrophobic all at once. To Bree, it felt like entering the tent of a sheikh's harem. But as she approached the wealthy men who were playing at the single large table, if there was a stab of fear down her spine, she didn't feel it.

She'd succeeded. She'd turned off her heart.

There were no women players. The only females in the room stood in a circle behind the men, smiling with hawkish red lips, wearing low-cut, tight silk gowns. At the table, she saw the dealer, Chris—what was his last name?—whose eyes widened with surprise when he saw her

The four players at the table were Greg Hudson and three owners she recognized: a Belgian land developer, a long-mustached oil man from Texas and a short, bald tycoon from Silicon Valley. But where was the arrogant stranger Josie had mentioned? Had he already quit the game?

Whatever. It was time to play.

In her black leather jacket and jeans, Bree pushed through the venomous, overdressed women. Without a word, she sat down at one of the two empty seats at the table around the dealer, beside Greg Hudson.

"Deal me in," she said coolly.

The men blinked, staring at her in shock that was almost comical. One of the men snorted a laugh. Another frowned. "Another cocktail waitress?" one scoffed.

"Actually," Bree said with a grin, "I'm with the housekeeping staff, and so was my sister."

The men glanced at each other uncertainly.

"Well, well. Bree Dalton." Greg Hudson licked his lips, looking at her with beady eyes in his florid, sweaty face. "So. Did you bring the hundred thousand dollars your sister owes me?"

"You know we don't have that kind of money."

"Then I'll send my men to take it out of her hide."

Bree's knees shook beneath the table, but she did not feel fear. Her body might feel whatever it liked, but she'd disconnected it from her heart. Crossing her legs, she leaned back in her chair. "I will play for her debt."

"You!" He snorted. "What will you wager? This game has a five-thousand-dollar buy-in. You could scrub the bathrooms of the entire Hale Ka'nani Resort for years and not have that kind of money."

"I offer a trade."

"You have nothing of value."

"I have myself."

Her boss stared at her, then licked his lips. "You mean—"

"Yes. I mean you could have me in bed." She looked at him steadily, feeling nothing. Her skin felt cold, her heart as frozen as the blue iceberg that sank the *Titanic*. "You wanted me, Mr. Hudson. Here I am."

There was a low whistle, an intake of breath around the room.

Bree slowly gazed around the table. She had everyone's complete attention. Without flinching, she let her gaze taunt each man in turn, all of them larger, older and more powerful than she could ever be. "Who will take the gamble?"

"Well now." Looking her over, the Texas oil baron thoughtfully tilted back his cowboy hat. "This game just got a lot more interesting."

In the corner of her eye, she saw a dark, hulking shadow come around the table. A man sat down in the empty chair on the other side of the dealer, and Bree instantly turned to him with languid eyes. "Allow me to join your game, and I could be yours…."

Bree's voice choked off midsentence as she sucked in her breath.

She knew those cold blue eyes. The high cheekbones, sharp as a razor blade. The strong jaw that proclaimed ruthless, almost thuggish strength. So powerful, so darkly handsome, so sensual.

So impossible.

"No," she whispered. Not after ten years. Not here. "It can't be."

Vladimir Xendzov's eyes narrowed with recognition, and then she felt the rush of his sudden searing hatred like fire.

"Have you met Prince Vladimir?" Greg Hudson purred.

"Prince?" Bree choked out. She was unable to look away from Vladimir's face, the face of the man she'd dreamed about unwillingly for the past ten years.

His cruel, sensual lips curved as he leaned back in his chair. "Miss Dalton," he drawled. "I didn't know you were in Hawaii. And gambling. What a pleasant surprise."

His low, husky voice, so close to her, so real, caused a shiver across her skin. She stared at him in shock.

Her one lost love. Not a ghost. Not a dream. But here, at the Hale Ka'nani Resort, not six feet away from her.

"So what's on offer? Your body, is it?" Vladimir's words were cold, even sardonic. "What a charming prize that would be, though hardly exclusive. Shared by thousands, I should imagine."

And just like that, the ice around her heart exploded into a million glass splinters. She sucked in her breath.

Vladimir Xendzov had made her love him with all the reckless passion of an innocent, untamed heart. He'd made her a better person—and then he'd destroyed her. Her lips parted. "Vladimir."

He stiffened. *"Your Highness* will do."

She didn't realize she'd spoken his name aloud. Glancing to the right and left, she matched his sardonic tone. "So you're using your title now."

His blue eyes burned through her. "It is mine by right."

She knew it was true. His great-grandfather had been one of the last great princes of Russia, before he'd died fighting the Red Army in Siberia, after sending his wife and baby son to safety in Alaskan exile. As a poverty-stricken child, Vladimir had been mocked with the title at school. When he was twenty-five, he'd told her that he never intended to use the title, that it still felt like a mockery, an honor he hadn't earned—and was worthless, anyway.

But apparently, now, he'd found a use for it.

"You didn't always think so," Bree said.

"I am no longer the boy you once knew," he said coldly.

She swallowed. Ten years ago, she'd thought Vladimir was the last honest man on earth. She'd loved him enough to give up the wicked skills that made her special. When he'd held her tight on a cold Alaskan night and begged her to be his bride, it had been the happiest night of her life. Then he'd ruthlessly deserted her the next morning, before she could tell him the truth. When she needed him most, he'd stabbed her in the back. Some *prince.* "What are you doing here?"

His lip curled. Without answering her, he turned away. "The table is full," he said to the other players. "We do not want her."

"Speak for yourself," one of them muttered, looking at Bree.

Looking around, she jolted in her chair. She'd forgotten the other men were there, looking at her like hungry wolves at a raw mutton chop. The beautiful, sexily dressed women standing in a circle behind them were glaring as if they would like to tear her limb from limb. Perhaps she'd taken her act a little too far.

Feel nothing, she ordered her shivering heart. *I have ice for a heart.* She looked away from the large, powerful men and sharp-taloned women. They couldn't hurt her. The only man who'd ever been able to really hurt her was Vladimir. And what more could he do, that he hadn't done already?

One thing, a cold voice whispered. Ten years ago, he'd taken her heart and soul.

But not her virginity.

And he never would, she told herself fiercely. Bree didn't know what Vladimir Xendzov was doing in Honolulu, but she didn't care. He was ancient history. All that mattered now was protecting Josie.

To save her little sister, Bree would play cards with the devil himself.

With an intake of breath, she lifted her chin, ignoring Vladimir as she looked around the table. "It is for this first game only that I offer my body. If I lose, the winner will get me, along with all the money in the pot. But if I win—" *when* I win, she amended silently "—I will only bet money. Until I possess the entire amount of my sister's debt."

As she spoke, her heart started to resume a normal beat. Bluffing, playing card games, was home to her. She'd learned poker when her father had pulled her up to their table in Anchorage and taught her at the tender age of four. By six, shortly after her mother had died two months after giving birth to Josie, Bree was a child prodigy accompanying her father to games—and, when he saw how much money she could make, his partner in crime.

Leaning forward, she looked at each man in turn, ignoring the death stares of the women behind them. "What is your answer?"

"We are here to play poker," another man complained. "Not for hookers."

Bree twirled her long blond hair slowly around one of her slender fingers and looked through her lashes at the Silicon Valley tycoon. "You don't recognize me, do you, Mr. McNamara?"

"Should I?"

She gave him a smile. "I guess not. But you knew my father, Black Jack Dalton." She paused. "Have you enjoyed the painting you paid him to steal from the archives of the Getty Museum in Los Angeles? When did you learn it was a fake?"

The Silicon Valley tycoon stiffened.

"And Mr. Vanderwald—" she turned to the gray-haired, overweight man sitting beside her boss "—twelve years ago you were nearly wiped out, weren't you? Investing in an Alaskan oil well that never existed."

The Belgian land developer scowled. "How the devil did you—"

"You thought my father conned you. But it was my idea. It was me," she whispered, lowering her eyelashes as she ran her hand down the softly worn leather of her black motorcycle jacket. "It was all me."

"You," the fat man breathed, staring at her.

She was doing well. Then, from the corner of her eye, she felt Vladimir's sardonic gaze. It hit her cheek and the side of her neck like a blast of ice. Her heart skidded with the effort it took to ignore him. He was the one man who'd ever really known her. The mark she'd stupidly let see behind her mask. She felt his hatred. Felt his scorn.

Fine. She felt the same about him. Let him hate her. His hatred bounced off the thickening ice of her scorn for *him*. She'd thought he was so perfect and noble. She'd killed herself trying to be worthy. But when he'd learned the truth about her past, he'd deserted her, without giving her a chance to explain.

So much for his honor. So much for his *love*.

Bree's lips twisted. Turning away, she gave the rest of the men a sensual smile. "Win this first hand, and you'll have me at your mercy. You'll get your revenge. Humiliate me completely. Take my body, and make your last memory of me one of your own pleasure." She gave a soft sigh, allowing her lips to part. "My skills at cards are nothing compared to what I can do to you in bed. I've learned the art of seduction. You have no idea," she whispered, "what I can do to you. A single hour with me will change your life."

Her act was one hundred percent fraud, of course. She, know the art of seduction? What a joke. She'd have no clue what she'd do with a man in bed. Since Vladimir, she'd been very careful never to let any man close to her. At twenty-eight, she was a virgin. But she did know how to bluff.

The men were riveted.

"I'm in," Greg Hudson croaked.

"And me."

"I accept."

"Yes."

As the men at the table agreed, Bree would have been frightened by all the looks of lust and desire and rage, if she hadn't frozen her heart against emotion.

But the last set of ice-blue eyes held no lust. No desire for domination. Just pure, cold understanding. As if Vladimir alone could see through all her tricks to the scared woman beneath.

"As you wish," he said softly. He gave a cold smile. "Let's play."

His low, sensual voice slid through her body. When she looked into Vladimir's eyes, fear pierced her armor. *Pierced her heart.* She wanted to leap up and run from his knowing gaze, to keep running and never stop. It took every ounce of her willpower to remain in the chair.

Clutching her jacket around her for warmth, she wrenched her gaze away, gripping the black leather so no one could see that her hands were shaking. "Then let's begin."

At Greg Hudson's nod, Chris the dealer dealt the cards. Ignoring the spiteful whispers and daggered glances of the trophy girls, Bree stared at her cards, facedown on the table.

She couldn't let herself think what would happen if she lost. Couldn't even imagine what it would be like to let any of these angry, fat, ugly men take their revenge on her virginal body through rough sex.

But even more awful would be having Vladimir win. Giving her virginity to the man who'd once broken her completely? She couldn't survive it. Not from him.

Just win, she ordered herself. All she had to do was take this first hand, and her virginity would no longer be on offer. It would be a long night of poker trying to win a hundred thousand dollars. But this was the most important hand.

Closing her eyes, she silently prayed. Then she picked up the cards. Careful not to let any of the players see them, she looked at them.

It took every ounce of her skill not to gasp.

Three kings. She had three kings, along with a four and a

queen. Three kings. She nearly wept with relief. It was as if
fate had decided she was gambling for the right reasons and
deserved to win.

Unless it was more than fate…

She looked up through her lashes toward the young dealer.
Could he be helping her? Chris was about Josie's age, and he'd
come twice to their apartment for dinner. He wasn't exactly a
close friend, but he'd spoken many times with irritation about
Greg Hudson's poor management skills. "You would do a better job of running this resort, Bree," he'd grumbled, and she'd
agreed with a smile. "But who wouldn't?"

Now, catching her eye, the young dealer gave her a wink
and a smile.

Sucking in her breath, Bree looked away before anyone noticed. Her eyes accidentally fell on Vladimir's. His eyebrows
lowered, and she gulped, looking back down at her cards, hast-
ily making her expression blank. Had he seen? Could he guess?

The dealer turned to his left. "Your Highness?"

Because of his placement at the table, Vladimir was the
first one required to add a bet to the pile of chips already in
the middle of the table from the ante. "Raise."

Raise? Bree looked up in surprise. He was looking straight
at her as he said, "Five thousand."

Texas Big-Hat cursed and threw his cards on the table.
"Fold."

"Call," Silicon Valley said, matching Vladimir's bet.

"Call," Mr. Vanderwald puffed, a bead of sweat dripping
down his forehead.

"Call," Greg Hudson said.

All eyes turned to Bree.

"She's already all in," Greg Hudson said dismissively.
"There's nothing more she can wager."

He was right, she thought with a pang. She couldn't match
Vladimir's raise, and that meant even if she won the hand, she
couldn't win anything beyond the twenty-five thousand dollars'

worth of chips currently in the center. What a waste of three kings…

Bree suddenly smiled. "I call."

"Call?" Greg Hudson hooted. "You have an extra five thousand dollars hidden in the back pocket of those jeans?"

She stretched back her shoulders and felt the eyes of the men linger on the shape of her breasts beneath her black T shirt. "I can match the bet in other ways. Instead of just an hour in bed, I'll offer an entire night." She tilted back her head, allowing her long blond hair to tumble provocatively down her shoulders. "Many chances. Multiple positions. As fast or slow or hard as you like it, all night long, and each time better than the last. Against the wall. Bent over the bed. In my mouth."

She felt like a total fool. She hoped she sounded like a woman who knew what she was talking about, not a scared virgin whose idea of lovemaking was vague at best, based only on movies and novels. But as she looked at each man at the table they seemed captivated. She exhaled. Her mask was holding. She was convincing them. Even Chris the dealer looked entranced.

Vladimir alone seemed completely unaffected. Bored, even. His lips twisted with scorn. And his eyes—

His blue eyes saw straight through her. A hot blush burned her cheeks as she said to him, "Do you agree my bet is commensurate with your five thousand dollar raise?"

"No," Vladimir said coldly. "That is not a call."

Her heart sank. "You…"

He gave her a calm smile. "That is an additional raise."

"A…a raise?" she echoed uncertainly.

"Obviously. Let us say…your added services are equivalent to an additional five thousand dollars? Yes. A full night with you would surely be worth that." He lifted a dark eyebrow. "Would you not agree?"

"Five thousand more?" Greg Hudson's voice hit a false note.

Catching himself, he shifted uncomfortably in his chair and snickered, "Fine with me. I'm half *raised* already."

"Good," Vladimir said softly, never looking away from Bree. "So we are in agreement."

Bree's brow furrowed as she tried to read his expression. What on earth was he doing?

Trying to help her? Or giving her more rope to hang herself with?

Repressing her inner tumult, she stared him down. *In for a penny...* She lifted her chin. "If it's worth five more, then why not ten more?"

The corners of Vladimir's mouth lifted. "Yes, indeed. Why not?" He looked around the table. "Miss Dalton has raised the wager by ten thousand dollars."

To her shock, one by one the men agreed to her supposed "raise," except for the Belgian, who folded with an unintelligible curse.

And just like that—oh, merciful heavens—there was suddenly a pile of chips at the center of the table worth *seventy-five thousand dollars.*

She looked at each man as they discarded cards and got new ones.

Don't play the hand, her father had always said. *Play the man.*

She forced herself to look across the table at Vladimir. His face was inscrutable as he discarded a card and got a new one. When she'd played him ten years ago, he'd had a tight style of play. He did not bluff, he did not overbet—the exact opposite of Bree's strategy.

He lifted his eyes to hers, and against her will, her heart turned over in her chest. His handsome face revealed nothing. The poverty of his homesteading Alaskan childhood, so different from hers, had pushed him to create a billion-dollar business across the world, primarily in metals and diamonds. He was so ruthless he had cut his own younger brother out of their partnership right before a multimillion-dollar deal. It was said Vladimir Xendzov had molten gold in his veins and a flinty diamond instead of a heart. That he wasn't flesh and blood.

But if Bree closed her eyes, she could still remember their last night together, when they'd almost made love on a bear-skin rug beneath the Christmas tree. She could remember the heat and searing pleasure of his lips against her skin in the deep hush of that cold winter's night.

I love you, Breanna. As I've never loved anyone.

No one else had ever called Bree by her full name. Not like that. Now, as they looked at each other across the poker table, they were two enemies with battle lines drawn. Everything she'd ever thought him to be was a dream. All that was left was a savagely handsome man with hard blue eyes and an emotionless face.

She turned away. Greg Hudson and the Silicon Valley tycoon were far easier to read. She watched her boss get three new cards, saw the sweat on his face and the way he licked his thick, rubbery lips as he stared down at his hand. Hudson had nothing. A pair of twos, maybe.

She looked at Silicon Valley. His lips were tight, his eyes irritated as he stared down moodily at his cards. He was probably already thinking about the twenty thousand dollars he'd wagered in the pot. She hid a smile.

"Miss Dalton?" Chris the dealer said. Stone-faced, she handed in the four of spades. Waited. And got back…

A queen.

She forced herself not to react, not even to breathe. Three kings and two queens. *A full house.*

It was an almost unbeatable hand. Careful not to meet Vladimir's eyes, she placed her cards facedown on the table. How she wished she could raise again! If only she had more to offer, she could have finished off her sister's debt right now— with a single hand!

Don't be greedy, she ordered herself. Seventy-five thousand dollars was plenty. Once she had it safely in her possession, the offer of her body—and unbeknownst to the men, her virginity—would be off the table.

But still. A full house. Her heart filled with regret.

"Raise," Vladimir said.

She looked up with a frown. Why would he raise now?

His eyes met hers. "Fifteen thousand."

"Fold." With a growl, Silicon Valley tossed his cards on the table. "Damn you."

Greg Hudson nervously wiped his forehead. For several seconds, he stared at his cards. Then he said in a small voice, "Call."

They all looked at her. Bree hesitated. She wanted to match Vladimir's raise. *Yearned* to. She had an amazing hand, and the amount now in the pot was even more than her sister's debt. But without anything more to offer, she was already all in. Even if she won, she wouldn't get the additional amount.

If only she had something more to offer!

"Well?" Vladimir's eyes met hers. "Will you call? Perhaps," he said in a sardonic voice, "you wish to raise your offer to an entire *weekend* of your charms?"

Bree stared at him in shock. A weekend?

She didn't know why he was helping her—or if he thought he could hurt her. But with this hand, it didn't matter. She was going to win.

"Great idea," she said coolly. "I'll match your raise with a full weekend of my—how did you put it? My charms?"

Vladimir's lips turned up slightly at the edges, though his eyes revealed nothing.

Heart pounding, she waited for Greg Hudson to object. But he didn't even look up. He just kept staring at his own cards, chewing on his lower lip.

It was time to reveal cards. Vladimir, based on his position at the table, went first. Slowly, he turned over his cards. He had two pairs—sevens and nines.

Relief flooded through Bree, making her body almost limp. She hadn't realized until that moment how scared she'd been that even with her completely unbeatable hand, Vladimir might find a way to beat her.

Greg Hudson's cards, on the other hand, were a foregone conclusion. He muttered a curse as he revealed a pair of threes.

Blinking back tears, Bree turned over her cards to reveal her full house, the three kings and two queens. There was a smattering of applause, exclamations and cursing across the room. She nearly wept as she reached for the pile of chips at the center of the table.

She'd saved Josie.

She'd won.

Bree's legs trembled beneath her as she rose unsteadily to her feet, swaying in her high-heeled stiletto boots. She pushed the bulk of the chips toward Greg Hudson, keeping only a handful for herself. "This pays my sister's debt completely, yes? We are free of you now?"

"Free?" Greg Hudson glared at her, then his piggy eyes narrowed. "Yes, you're free. In fact, I want you and your sister off this property tonight."

"You're firing us?" Her jaw dropped. "For what cause?"

"I don't need one," he said coldly.

She stiffened. She hadn't seen that coming. She should have. A small-minded man like her boss would never stand being beaten in a card game by a female employee. He'd already resented her for weeks, for the respect she'd quickly gained from the staff, and all the notes she'd left in the suggestion box, listing possible ways to improve his management of the resort.

"Fine." She grabbed her handful of chips and glared at him. "Then I'll tell you what I should have written up in the suggestion box weeks ago. This resort is a mess. You're being overcharged by your vendors, half your employees are stealing from you and the other half are ready to quit. You couldn't manage your way out of a paper bag!"

Mr. Hudson's face went apoplectic. "You—"

She barely heard him as he cursed at her. These extra chips, worth thousands of dollars, would give both Dalton girls a new start—buy them a plane trip back to the Mainland, first and last months' rent on a new apartment, and a little something extra to save for emergencies. And she would go someplace where she'd be sure she never, ever saw Vladimir Xendzov again. "I'll just cash in these chips, collect our last paychecks, and we'll be on our way."

"Wait, Miss Dalton," Vladimir said from behind her in a low, husky voice.

Her body obeyed, without asking her brain. Slowly, she turned. She couldn't help herself.

He was sitting calmly at the table, looking up at her with heavily lidded eyes. "I wish to play one more game with you."

Nervousness rose in her belly, but she tossed her head. "So desperate to win your money back? Are times so tough for billionaires these days?"

He smiled, and it did not meet his eyes. "A game for just the two of us. Winner take all."

"Why would I do that?"

Vladimir indicated his own entire pile of chips. "For this."

The blood rushed from her head, making her dizzy. "*All* of that?" she gasped.

He gave her a single nod.

Greg Hudson made a noise like a squeak. Sweat was showing through his tropical cotton shirt as he, along with everyone in the room, stared at the pile of chips. "But Prince Vladimir— Your Highness—that's a million dollars," he stammered.

"So it is," he replied mildly, as if the amount were nothing at all—and to Vladimir, it probably wasn't.

A single bead of sweat broke out between Bree's breasts. "And what would you want from me?"

His blue eyes seared right through her. "If I win," he said quietly, "you would be mine. For as long as I want you."

As long as he wanted her? "That would make me your… your slave."

Vladimir gave her a cold smile. "It is a wager I offer. You. For a million dollars."

"But that's—"

"Make your choice. Play me or go."

She swallowed, hearing a roar of blood in her ears.

"You can't just buy her!" her ex-boss brayed.

"That's up to Miss Dalton," Vladimir said. He turned his laserlike gaze on Bree. "So?"

Though there were ten other people in the room, it was so quiet she could have heard a pin drop. All eyes were on her.

A million dollars. The choice she made in this moment would determine the rest of her life—and Josie's. They could pay off their father's old debts to unsavory men, the ones that had kept them in virtual hiding for the past ten years. Josie would be free to go to college—any college she wanted. And Bree could start her own little B and B by the sea.

They'd no longer have to hide or be afraid.

They'd be free.

"What is the game?" she said weakly. "Poker?"

"Let's keep it easy. Leave it to fate. One card."

Her eyes widened. "One…"

His gorgeous face and chilly blue eyes revealed nothing as his sensual lips curved. "Are you feeling lucky, Miss Dalton?"

Was she feeling lucky?

Taking a million dollars from Vladimir would be more than sweet revenge. It would be justice for how he'd coldly abandoned her when she'd needed him most. He'd destroyed ten years of her life. She could take this one thing from him. A new life for her and Josie.

But risk being Vladimir's slave—forever? The thought made her body turn to ice. It was too much to risk on a random card from the deck.

Unless…it wasn't so random.

She looked sideways beneath her lashes at Chris, the dealer. He lowered his head, his expression serious. Was that a nod? Did she have a sympathetic ally? She closed her eyes.

How much was she willing to risk on a single card?

Are you feeling lucky, Miss Dalton?

Bree exhaled. She'd just won a hundred thousand dollars in a single game. She slowly opened her eyes. So, yes, she felt lucky. She sat back down at the table.

"I accept your terms," she stated emphatically.

Vladimir's smile widened. "So to be clear. If my card is higher, you'll belong to me, obeying my every whim, for as long as I desire."

"Yes," she said, glancing again at Chris. "And if mine is higher, you will give me every chip on that table."

"Agreed." Vladimir lifted a dark eyebrow. "Ace card high?"

"Yes."

They stared at each other, and Bree again forgot there was anyone else in the room. Until someone coughed behind her, and she jumped, realizing she'd been holding her breath.

Vladimir turned to the dealer. "Shuffle the deck."

Bree put the chips she'd won in the last game into a little pile and pushed them aside. "I will select my own card."

Her opponent looked amused. "I would expect no less."

They both turned to Chris, who visibly gulped. Shuffling carefully, with all eyes upon him, he fanned out the facedown cards. He turned them toward Bree, who made her selection, then toward Vladimir, who did the same.

Holding her breath, Bree slowly turned her card over.

The king of hearts.

She'd drawn the king of hearts! She'd won!

She gasped aloud, no longer able to control her emotions. Flipping her card onto the table to reveal the suit, she covered her face with her palms and sobbed with joy. After ten years, fate had brought the untouchable Vladimir Xendzov into her hands, to give her justice at last. Parting her hands, she lifted her gaze, waiting for the sweetness of the moment when he turned over his own losing card, and his face fell as he realized he'd lost and she'd won.

Vladimir looked down at his card. For an instant, his hard expression didn't change.

Then he looked up at her and smiled. A real smile that reached his eyes.

It was an ice pick through her heart.

"Sorry, Bree," he said casually, and tossed his card onto the table.

She stared down at the ace of diamonds.

Her mind went blank. Then a tremble went through her, starting at her toes and moving up her body as she looked at Vladimir, her eyes wide and uncomprehending. She dimly heard Greg Hudson's annoyed curse and the other men's cheers, heard the women's snide laughter—except for the woman directly behind Vladimir, who seemed to be crying.

"You—you've…" Bree couldn't speak the words.

"I've won." Vladimir looked at her, his blue eyes electric with dislike. He rose from his chair, all six feet four inches of him, and said coldly, "You have ten minutes to pack. I will collect my winnings in the lobby." As she gaped at him, he walked around the table to stand over her, so close she could feel the warmth of his body. He leaned nearer, his face inches from hers.

"I've waited a long time for this," he said softly. "But now, at last, Bree Dalton—" his lips slid into a hard, sensual smile "—you are mine."

CHAPTER TWO

BREE'S heart stopped in her chest.

As Vladimir turned away, she struggled to wake up from this bad dream. She looked down at her overturned card on the table. The king of hearts looked back at her. Bree should have won. She was supposed to win. Her brain whirled in confusion.

"Wake up," she whispered to herself. But it wasn't a dream. She'd just sold herself. Forever. To the only man she hated.

Blinking, she looked up tearfully at the young dealer, who she'd thought was her ally. Chris just shook his head. "Wow," he said in awe. "That was a really stupid bet."

Bree gripped the edge of the table with trembling hands. Staggering to her feet, she turned on Vladimir savagely. "You cheated!"

From the doorway, he whirled back to face her. *"Cheated?"*

He went straight toward her, and the crowds parted for him, falling back from his powerful presence and his expression of fury. He looked as cold as a marble statue, like an ancient tsar of perfect masculine beauty, of despotic strength and ruthless cruelty. He reached for her, and she backed away, terrified of the look in his eyes.

Vladimir dropped his hands. His posture relaxed and his voice became a sardonic drawl. "You are the one who cheats, my dear. And you'd best hurry." He glanced at his platinum watch. "You now only have—nine minutes to pack before I collect my prize."

She gasped aloud. His *prize?*

Her body—her soul!

Turning without another word, Vladimir stalked out the door with a warrior's easy, deadly grace. Everyone in the room, Bree included, remained silent until the door closed behind him. Then the crowd around her burst into noise, and Bree's knees went weak. She leaned her trembling hands against the table. Her ex-boss was yelling something in her ear: "Nine minutes is too long. I want you out of the Hale Ka'nani in five!"

Greg Hudson looked as if he were dying to slap her across the face. But she knew he couldn't touch her. Not now. Not ever.

She was Vladimir Xendzov's property now.

How could she have been so stupid? How?

Bree had never hated herself so much as she did in that moment. She rubbed her eyes, hard. She'd thought she could save her hapless baby sister from the perils of gambling. Instead, she'd proved herself more stupidly naive than Josie had ever been.

The warm, close air in the red-curtained, windowless room suddenly choked her. Pushing past the annoyed blonde who'd stood behind Vladimir's chair, Bree ran for the exit, past a startled Kai who was guarding the door. She rushed down the hall, past the deserted outdoor bar, into the dark night.

She ran up the hill, trying to focus on the feel of the path beneath her feet, on the hard rhythm of her breathing. But she was counting down her freedom in minutes. Eight. Seven and a half. Seven.

Her right foot stumbled and she slowed to a walk, her breath a rasp in her throat. The moon glowed above her as she reached the apartment building she shared with her sister.

Bree shivered as a warm breeze blew against her clammy skin. Rushing up the open-air stairs of the aged, moss-covered structure, she shook with fear. He would take everything from her. Everything.

She'd been stupid. So stupid. He'd set his trap and she'd

walked right into it. And now Josie would be left alone, with no one to watch out for her.

Bree started to reach for the doorknob, then stopped. Her body shook as she remembered the poker chips she'd been so proud to win—all of which she'd left behind. With a choked sob, she covered her face with her hands. How would she ever explain this disaster to Josie?

The door abruptly opened.

"There you are," Josie said. "I saw you come up the path. Did you manage to…?" But her sister's hopeful voice choked off when she saw Bree's face. "Oh," she whispered. "You… you lost?"

Josie spoke the words as if they were impossible. As if she'd never once thought such a thing could happen. Bree had never lost big like this before—ever. Even tonight, she would have won, if she hadn't allowed Vladimir to tempt her into one last game. Her hands clenched at her sides. She didn't know who she hated more at this moment—him or herself.

Him. Definitely him.

"What happened?" Josie breathed.

"The stranger was Vladimir," Bree said through dry lips. "The man who kicked you out of the game was Vladimir Xendzov."

Josie stared at her blankly. But of course—she'd been only twelve when their father had died, and Bree had set her sights on the twenty-five-year-old businessman with a small mining company, who'd returned to Alaska to try to buy back his family's land. She'd hoped to con him out of enough cash to pay off the dangerous men who'd tracked them down and were demanding repayment of the money Black Jack and Bree had once stolen.

She'd fallen for Vladimir instead. And Christmas night, when he'd proposed to her, she'd decided to tell him everything. But his brother told him first—and by then, it was in the newspapers. Without a word, he'd abruptly left Alaska, leaving eighteen-year-old Bree and her sister threatened by dangerous men—as well as the sheriff, who'd wanted to toss Bree into jail and Josie into foster care. So they'd thrown everything into their beat-up old car in the middle of the night, and headed south. For the past ten years, they'd never stopped running.

"You lost? At poker?" Josie repeated, dazed. Her eyes suddenly welled up with tears. "This is all my fault."

"It's not your fault," Bree said tightly.

"Of course it is!"

Josie was clearly miserable. Looking at her little sister's tearful face, Bree came to a sudden decision. She grabbed her duffel bag.

"Pack," she said tersely.

Josie didn't move. Her expression was bewildered. "Where are we going?"

Bree stuffed her passport into her bag, and any clean clothes she could reach. "Airport. You have two minutes."

"Oh, my God," Josie breathed, staring at her. "You want to run. What on earth did you lose?"

"Move!" Bree barked.

Jumping, her sister turned and grabbed her knapsack. A scant hundred seconds later, Bree was pulling on her hand and yanking her toward the door.

"Hurry." She flung open the door. "We'll get our last paychecks and—"

Vladimir stood across the open-air hallway. His broadshouldered, powerful body leaned casually against the wall in the shadows.

"Going somewhere?" he murmured silkily.

Bree stopped short, staring up in shock. Behind her, Josie ran into her back with a surprised yelp.

He lifted a dark eyebrow and gave Bree a cold smile. "I had a feeling you would attempt to cheat me. But I admit I'm disappointed. Some part of me had hoped you might have changed over the last ten years."

Other hulking shadows appeared on the stairs. He hadn't come alone.

Desperately, Bree tossed her head and glared at him defiantly. "How do you know I wasn't just hurrying to be on time to meet you in the lobby?"

Vladimir's smile became caustic. "Hurrying to meet me? No. Ten years ago you could barely be on time for anything. You'd have been late to my funeral."

"Oh, I'd be early for your funeral, believe me! Holding flowers and red balloons!"

His blue eyes gleamed as he came toward her in the shadows. She felt Josie quivering behind her, so as he reached for her, Bree forced herself not to flinch or back away.

"People don't change," he said softly. He pulled the duffel bag from her shoulder. Unzipping it, he turned away from her, and she exhaled. Then, as he went through the bag, she glared at him.

"What do you think I have in there—a rifle or something? Didn't anyone ever tell you it's rude to go through other people's stuff?"

"A woman like you doesn't need a rifle. You have all the feminine weapons you need. Beauty. Seduction. Deceit." Vladimir gazed at her with eyes dark as a midnight sea. His handsome, chiseled face seemed made of granite. "A pity your charms don't work on me."

As she looked at him, her throat tightened. She whispered, "If you despise me so much, just let me go. Easier for you. Easier for everyone."

His lips curved. "Is that the final item on your checklist?"

"What are you talking about?"

"You've tried running, insulting me, accusing me of cheating, and now you're *reasoning* with me." Zipping up the bag, he pushed it back into her arms and looked at her coldly. "What's next—begging for mercy?"

She held the bag over her heart like a shield. "Would it

work?" she breathed. "If I begged you—on my knees—would you let me go?"

Reaching out, Vladimir cupped her cheek. He looked down at her almost tenderly. "No."

She jerked her chin away. "I hate you!"

Vladimir gave a low, bitter laugh. "So you did have a checklist. It's fascinating, really, how little you've changed."

If only that were true, Bree thought. She didn't have a plan. She was going on pure instinct. Ten years of living a scrupulously honest life, of scraping to get by on minimum-wage jobs, and taking care of her sister, had left Bree's old skills of sleight of hand and deception laughably out-of-date. She was rusty. She was clumsy and awkward.

And Vladimir made it worse. He brought out her weakness. She couldn't hide her feelings, even though she knew it would be to her advantage to cloak her hatred. But he'd long ago learned the secret ways past the guarded walls of her heart.

"You can't be serious about making me your slave forever!" she snapped.

"What?" Josie gasped, clinging to her arm.

Vladimir's eyes were hard in the moonlight. "You made the bet. Now you will honor it."

"You tricked me!"

He gave her a lazy smile. "You thought that dealer was going to stick his neck out for you, didn't you? But men don't sacrifice themselves for women anymore. Not even for pretty ones." He moved closer to her, leaning his head down to her ear. "I know all your tells, Bree," he whispered. "And soon… I will know every last secret of your body."

Bree felt the warmth of his breath on her neck, felt the brush of his lips against the tender flesh of her earlobe. Prickles raced through her, making her hair stand on end as he towered over her. She felt tiny and feminine compared to his powerful masculine strength, and against her will, she licked her lips as a shiver went down her body.

Vladimir straightened, and his eyes glittered like an arctic sea. "This time, you will fulfill your promises."

He made a small movement with his hand, and the three shadows on the stairs came forward, toward the bare light outside their apartment. Vladimir strode down the steps without looking back, leaving his three bodyguards to corral the two Dalton sisters and escort them down the concrete staircase.

Two luxury vehicles waited in the dimly lit parking lot. The first was a black SUV with tinted windows. The second... Bree's feet slowed.

"Bree!"

Hearing her sister's panicked voice behind her, she turned around and saw the bodyguards pushing Josie into the backseat of the SUV.

Bree clenched her hands as she went forward. "Let her go!"

Vladimir grabbed her arm. "You're coming with me."

"I won't be separated from her!"

He looked at her, his face hard and oh, so handsome in the moonlight. "My Lamborghini only has two seats." When she didn't move, he said with exaggerated patience, "They will be right behind us."

Glancing at the SUV parked behind the Lamborghini, Bree saw her sister settled in the backseat as the bodyguards climbed in beside her. Bree ground her teeth. "Why should I trust you?"

"You have no choice."

He reached for her hand, but she ripped it away. "Don't touch me!"

Vladimir narrowed his eyes. "I was merely trying to be courteous. Clearly a waste." He thrust his thumb toward the door of the bright red Lamborghini. "Get in."

Opening the door, Bree climbed inside the car and took a deep breath of the soft leather seats' scent. Fast cars had once been her father's favorite indulgence, back when they'd been conning rich criminals across the West, and Black Jack had been spending money even faster than they made it. By the time her father died of lung cancer, only debts were left. But the smell of the car reminded her of the time when her father had been her hero and their mattresses had been stuffed with money—literally. Unwillingly, Bree ran her hand over the smooth leather.

"Nice car," she said grudgingly.

With a sudden low laugh, Vladimir started the engine. "It gets me where I need to go."

At the sound of that laugh, she sucked in her breath.

His laugh...

She'd first heard it at a party in Anchorage, when Vladimir Xendzov was just a mark, half owner of a fledgling mining company, who had come to Alaska looking to buy the land her father had left in an ironclad trust for Josie, then just twelve years old. Bree had been hoping she could distract Vladimir from the legal facts long enough to disappear with his money. Instead, when their eyes met across the room, she'd been electrified. He'd grabbed an extra flute of champagne and come toward her.

"I know who you are," he'd said.

She'd hid the nervous flutter in her belly. "You do?"

He gave her a wicked smile. "The woman who's coming home with me tonight."

For an instant, she'd caught her breath. Then she'd laughed in his face. "Does that line usually work?"

He'd looked surprised, then he'd joined her laughter with his own low baritone. "Yes," he'd said almost sheepishly. "In fact, it always does." He'd held out his hand with a grin. "Let's try this again. I'm Vladimir."

Now, as his eyes met hers, his expression was like stone. He yanked hard on the wheel of the Lamborghini, pulling the car away from the curb with a squeal of tires. Bree glanced behind them, and saw her sister's SUV was indeed following them. She exhaled.

She had to think of a way to get out of this prison sentence.

She looked at the passing lights of Honolulu. The city sparkled, even in the dead of night.

Deals can always be made. Her father's words came back to her. *Just figure out what a man wants most. And find a way to give it to him—or make him think you will.*

But what could a man like Vladimir possibly want, that he didn't already have?

He was frequently in the business news—and nearly as often in the tabloids. He was the sole owner of Xendzov Mining OAO, with operations on six continents. His company was one of the leading producers of gold, platinum and diamonds around the world. He was famous for his workaholic ways, for his lavish lifestyle, and most of all for the ruthless way he crushed his competition—most spectacularly his own brother, who'd once been part-owner of the company before Vladimir had forced him out, the same day he'd abandoned Bree in Alaska. For ten years, the two brothers' brutal, internecine battles had caused them both to lose millions of dollars, tarnishing both their reputations.

Ala Moana Boulevard was deserted as they drove away from Waikiki, heading toward downtown. Along the wide dark beach across the street, palm trees stretched up into the violet sky. They passed Ala Moana Center, which was filled with shops such as Prada, Fendi and Louis Vuitton—brands that Bree had once worn as a teenage poker player, but which as a hotel housekeeper she couldn't remotely afford. Vladimir could probably buy out the entire mall without flinching, she thought. Just as he'd bought her.

Bree rolled down her window to breathe the warm night air. "So tell me," she said casually. "What brings you to Honolulu?"

He glanced at her out of the corner of his eye. "Don't."

"What?"

"Play whatever angle you're hoping to use against me."

"I wasn't…"

"I can hear the purr in your voice." His voice was sardonic.

"It's the same one you used at the poker table, whipping the male players into a frenzy by offering your body as the prize."

Anger rushed through her, but she took a deep breath. He was right—that wasn't exactly her proudest moment. She looked down at her hands, clenched in her lap. "I was desperate. I had nothing else to offer."

"You weren't desperate when you played that last card against me. Your sister's debt was already paid. You could have walked away."

Tears burned the backs of her eyes. "You don't understand. We are in debt—"

"Fascinating." His voice dripped sarcasm.

Didn't he have even the slightest bit of humanity, even a sliver of a flesh-and-blood heart? Her throat ached as she looked away. "I can't believe I ever loved you."

"Loved?" Changing gears as they sped down the boulevard, he gave a hard laugh. "It's tacky to bring that up. Even for you."

Ahead of them, she saw the towering cruise ships parked like floating hotels at the pier. She blinked fast, her heart aching. She wished both she and Josie were on one of those ships, headed to Japan—or anywhere away from Vladimir Xendzov. She swallowed against the razor blade in her throat. "You can't be serious about taking me to bed."

"The deal was made."

"What kind of man accepts a woman's body as a prize in a card game?"

"What kind of woman offers herself?"

She gritted her teeth and blinked fast, staring at the Aloha Tower and the cruise ships. Without warning, Vladimir suddenly veered the Lamborghini to the right.

Glancing behind them, Bree saw the SUV with her sister continuing straight down the Nimitz Highway, a different direction from the Lamborghini. She turned to him with a gasp.

"Where are you taking my sister?"

Vladimir pressed down more firmly on the gas, zooming

at illegal speeds through the eerily empty streets of downtown Honolulu in the hours before dawn. "You should be more concerned about where I am taking you."

"You can't separate me from Josie!"

"And yet I have," he drawled.

"Take me back!"

"Your sister has nothing to do with this," he said coldly. "*She* did not wager her body."

Bree cursed at him with the eloquence of Black Jack Dalton himself, but Vladimir only glanced at her with narrowed eyes. "You have no power over me, Bree. Not anymore."

"No!" Desperate, she looked around for a handy police car—anything! But the road was empty, desolate in the darkest part of night before dawn. "I won't let you do this!"

"You'll soon learn to obey me."

She gasped in desperate fury. Then she did the only thing she could think of to make him stop the car. Reaching between the seats, she grabbed the hand brake and yanked upwards with all her might.

Bree's neck jerked back and tires squealed as the fast-moving car spun out of control.

As if in slow motion, she looked at Vladimir. She heard his low gasp, saw him fight the steering wheel, gripping until his knuckles were white. As the car spun in a hard circle, the colored lights of the city swirled around them, then shook in chaos when they bumped up over a curb. Bree screamed, throwing her hands in front of her face as the car plummeted toward a skyscraper of glass and steel.

The red Lamborghini abruptly pulled to a stop.

With a gulp, Bree slowly opened her eyes. When she saw how close they had come to hitting the office building, she sucked in her breath. Dazed, she reached her hand through the car's open window toward the plate glass window, just inches away, literally close enough for her to touch. If Vladimir weren't such a capable driver… If the car had gone a little more to the right…

They'd have crashed through the lobby of the skyscraper in an explosion of glass.

Her reckless desperation to save her sister had very nearly killed them both. Bree was afraid to look at him. She coughed, eyes watering from the cloud of dust that rose from the car's tires. She slowly turned.

Vladimir's silhouette was framed by a Gothic cathedral of stone and stained glass on the other side of the street. A fitting background for the dark avenging angel now glaring at her in deathly fury.

"The airport." His breathing was still heavy, his blue eyes shooting daggers of rage. "My men are taking your sister to the *airport,* damn you. Do you think I would hurt her?"

Heart in her throat, Bree looked back at him. "How would I know?"

He stared at her for a long moment. "You," he said coldly, "are the only one who's put her at risk. You, Bree."

As he restarted the car and drove down the curb, back onto the deserted road, a chill went down her spine.

Was he right?

She put her hand against her hot forehead. She'd spent ten years protecting her sister with all her heart, but from the moment she'd seen Vladimir, her every instinct was wrong. Every choice she made seemed to end in disaster. Maybe Josie *was* better off without her. "Your men will take her straight to the airport? Do you promise?"

"I promise nothing. Believe me or don't."

Bree's body still shook as they drove out of downtown, eventually leaving the city behind, heading north into the green-shadowed mountains at the center of the island. As they drove through the darkly green hills of Oahu, moonlight illuminated the low-slung clouds kissing the earth. She finally looked at him.

"Josie doesn't have any money for a plane ticket," she said in a small voice.

"My men will escort her onto one of my private jets, and she'll be taken back to the Mainland. A bodyguard already procured her last paycheck from the hotel. And yours, since you no longer need money."

Bree's mouth fell open. "I don't need money? Are you crazy?"

"You are my possession now. I will provide you with everything I feel you require."

"Oh," she said in a small voice. She bit her lip. "So you mean you'll feed me and house me? Like…like your pet?"

His hands tightened on the steering wheel. "A pet would imply affection. You are more like…a serf."

"A serf?" she gasped.

"Just as my ancestors once had in Russia." He looked at her. "For the rest of your life, you will work for me, Bree. For free. You will never be paid, or allowed to leave. Your only reason for living will be to serve me and give me pleasure."

Bree swallowed.

"Oh," she whispered. Good to know where she stood. Setting her jaw, she looked out at the spectacular vista of sharp hills on either side of the Pali Highway, then closed her eyes. At least Josie was free, Bree thought. At least she'd done one thing right before she disappeared forever.…

Her eyes flew open. *No.* She sat up straight in her seat. She wasn't going to give up so easily. She'd find a way to escape her fate. She *would!*

She folded her arms, glaring at him. "Where do you intend to hide me, Vladimir? Because I hardly think your shareholders would approve of slavery. Or *kidnapping.*"

"Kidnapping!" Vladimir spoke a low, guttural word in Russian that was almost certainly a curse. "After so many years of lies, do you even know how to tell the truth?"

"What else would you call it when you—"

"You had the money to pay your sister's debt. You were free to leave. But you chose to gamble out of pure greed. And now you're too much of a coward to admit you lost." He turned to her, his blue eyes like ice in the moonlight. "I let your sister go because you're the one I want to punish, Bree. Only you." He gave a slow, cold smile. "And I will."

CHAPTER THREE

VLADIMIR watched a tumult of emotions cross Bree's beautiful face. Rage. Fury. Grief. And most of all helplessness.

It was like Christmas and his birthday all at once.

Still smiling, he turned back to the deserted, moonlit road and pushed down on the gas of the Lamborghini, causing it to give a low purr as it sped through the lush mountains of Oahu's interior.

When he'd first seen young Josie Dalton at the poker game, getting lured in over her head by the hotel manager, he hadn't recognized her. How could he? He'd never met the kid before. He'd just thought some idiot girl was letting herself get played.

He hadn't liked it, so he'd tried to get her out of the game. An unusually charitable deed for a man who now prided himself on having a cold, flinty diamond instead of a heart.

Once, he'd tried to protect his younger brother. Once, he'd believed in the woman he loved. Now he despised weakness, especially in himself. But three months ago, after nearly dying in a fiery crash on the Honolulu International Raceway, he'd taken his doctor's advice and bought a beach house on a secluded stretch of the Windward Coast, to recuperate.

He'd had no clue Bree was in Hawaii. If he'd known, he'd have gotten up from his hospital bed and walked to the airport, broken bones and all. What man in his right mind would seek out Bree Dalton? That would be like yearning for a plague or other infectious disease.

She was poison, pure and simple. A poison that tasted sweet as sugar and spicy as cinnamon, but once ingested, would destroy a man's body from within, like acid. And that's just what she'd done ten years ago. Her scheming, callous heart had burned Vladimir so badly that she'd sucked all the mercy from his soul.

She'd done him a favor, really. He was better off without a working heart. Being free of sympathy or emotion had helped him build a worldwide business. Helped him get rid of a business partner he no longer wanted.

Bree had betrayed him. But so had his younger brother, in revealing that deception to a newspaper reporter while their first major deal was on the line. Burned, Vladimir had ruthlessly cut his brother out of their company, buying him out for pennies. Then he'd announced his acquisition of mining rights in a newly discovered gold field in northern Siberia. A year later, at twenty-six, Vladimir was worth five hundred million dollars, while his twenty-four-year-old brother was still broke and living in the Moroccan desert.

Though Kasimir hadn't remained penniless for long. Even living like a nomad in the Sahara, thousands of miles from the ice and snow, he'd found a way to start his own mining company, one that now rivaled Xendzov Mining OAO. Vladimir's eyes narrowed. He'd allowed Kasimir to peck away at his business for long enough. It was time for him to destroy his brother once and for all.

But first…

Vladimir's lips curled as he drove the Lamborghini through the hills toward the Windward Coast. He glanced at Bree out of the corner of his eye.

He'd told himself for years that his memory of her was wrong. No woman could possibly be that lovely, that enticing.

And it was true. She wasn't. At eighteen, she'd still been a girl.

Now, at twenty-eight, she was the most beautiful woman

he'd ever seen. Her fragility and mystery, mixed with her outward toughness, made her more seductive than ever.

And soon, he'd know her every secret. As they drove down the hills into a lush, green valley, a cold smile lifted Vladimir's lips. He would satisfy his hot memory of her—the thirst that, no matter how many cool blondes he took to his bed, still haunted him in dreams at night. He would satiate himself with her body.

He'd be disappointed by the experience, of course. His memory had amplified her into a goddess of desire. No woman could be that extraordinary. No woman could kiss that well. No woman could set such a fire in his blood. He'd built her up.

He would enjoy cutting her down.

From the moment Vladimir had heard her sultry voice at the poker table, and seen her slender, willowy body in the tight dark jeans and black leather jacket, her hazel eyes like a deep, mysterious forest and her full pink lips like the luring temptation into heaven—or hell—his every nerve ending had become electrified in a way he hadn't felt in a long, long time.

At first he'd thought it was fate. When she'd taken him up on his final bet, he'd realized the two Dalton sisters must have been working some kind of con. It was the only explanation. He could think of no other reason for Bree Dalton, the smartest, sexiest, most ruthless con artist he'd ever met, to be working as an underpaid housekeeper in a five-star Hawaiian resort.

But now he'd teach proud, wicked Bree a lesson she'd never forget. He'd have her as his slave. Scrubbing his floors. And most of all, pleasuring him in bed. He looked at her, at the way her long blond hair glowed in the moonlight, at the fullness of her breasts trembling with each angry breath. Oh, yes.

"Your girlfriend is going to hate you for this," she muttered.

In the distance, Vladimir could see the violet sky growing light pink over the vast dark Pacific. "I don't have a girlfriend."

She glared at him. "Yes, you do."

"Wouldn't I know?"

"What about the woman whose breasts were pressed against your back throughout the poker game?"

"Oh." He tilted his head. "You mean Heather."

"Right. Heather. Won't she object to this little master-slave thing with me?"

He shrugged. "I met her at the pool a few days ago. She was perhaps amusing for a moment, but…"

"But now you're done with her, so you're heartlessly casting her aside." Bree's jaw set as she turned away. "Typical."

"Do not worry. I have no intention of casting *you* aside," he assured her.

"A famous playboy like you? You'll tire of me in bed after the first night."

He found the hope in her voice insulting. Women did not wish to be cast out of his bed. They begged to get in. Hiding his irritation, he gave her a sensual smile. "Do not fear. If that happens, I'll find some other way for you to serve me. Scrubbing my floors. Cleaning my house…"

Her cheeks turned a girlish shade of pink, but her voice was steady as she said, "I'd rather clean your bathroom with my *toothbrush* than have you touch me."

"Perhaps I'll have you clean my house naked," he mused.

"Sounds like heaven," she muttered, tossing her head.

Driving along the edge of the coast, he stroked his chin with one hand. "Perhaps I'll allow my men to enjoy the show."

That finally got her. Bree's eyes went wide as her lips parted. "You…" She swallowed, looking pale. "You wouldn't."

Of course he wouldn't. Vladimir had no intention of sharing his hard-won prize—or even the image of her—with anyone. He wasn't much of a sharer, in any case. A man was stronger alone. With no gaps in his armor. With no one close enough to slow him down, or stab him in the back.

Looking away from Bree's pale, panicked face—somehow he didn't enjoy seeing that expression there as much as he'd thought he would—he turned the Lamborghini into the road to his ultraprivate, palatial Hawaii mansion. The guard nodded at him from the guardhouse and opened the ten-foot-tall electric gate.

"Relax, Bree." Vladimir ground out the words, keeping his eyes on the road. "I don't intend to share you. You're my prize and mine alone."

In the corner of his eye, he saw her tight shoulders relax infinitesimally. *This is supposed to be her punishment,* he mocked himself. *Why reassure her?*

But frightening her wasn't what he wanted, he decided. He had no interest in seeing her pitiful and terrified. He wanted to conquer the real Bree—proud and sly and gloriously beautiful. He didn't want to be tempted, even once, to feel sympathy for her.

Vladimir stopped the red car in the paved courtyard in front of his enormous beachside mansion, built on the edge of a cliff, with one story on the courtyard side, and three stories facing the ocean.

"This is yours?" she breathed.

"Yes."

"I didn't know you had a place on Oahu." She bit her lip, looking up at the house. "If I'd known you were here…"

"You wouldn't have come to Honolulu to try your con?"

"Con?" She looked genuinely shocked. "What are you talking about?"

"What do you call that poker game?"

Her big hazel eyes were wide and luminous in the moonlight.

"The worst mistake of my life," she whispered.

Her heart-shaped face was pale, her pink lips full, her expression agonized. In spite of her tough-girl clothes, the black leather jacket and stiletto boots, she looked like a young, lost princess, trapped by an ogre with no hope of escape.

A trick, he told himself angrily. *Don't fall for it.* He turned off the ignition. Grabbing her duffel bag, he got out of the car. "Come on."

Closing the door behind him, he stalked toward the front door without looking back. He'd bought this twenty-million-dollar house three months ago, sight unseen, an hour before he was released from the hospital in Honolulu. The lavish estate on the windward side of the Oahu shore was set on the best private beach near Kailua.

He went into the sprawling beach house, and heard the sound of her stiletto boots on the patterned ohia wood floor. They passed through the large, expansive rooms. Floor-to-ceiling windows on both sides of the house revealed the Ka'iwa Mountain Ridge in one direction, and in the other, the distant pink-and-lavender dawn breaking over the Pacific and the distant Mokulua Islands.

But Vladimir was used to the view. Sick of it, in fact. He'd spent weeks cooped up like a prisoner here, as he recuperated from the car race that had nearly killed him, gritting his teeth through physical therapy. No wonder, within a month of being here, he'd started seeking amusement in Honolulu, half an hour away, at a private poker game. The fact that it was illegal to gamble at any resort in Hawaii just added to the spice.

At the end of the hall, Vladimir opened double doors into the enormous master bedroom, revealing high ceilings, an elegant marble fireplace and a huge four-poster bed. Veranda doors opened to a balcony that overlooked the infinity pool and the ocean beyond it. He dropped Bree's duffel bag on the bed and abruptly turned to face her.

She ran straight into him.

Vladimir heard her intake of breath as, for one instant, he felt the softness of her body against his own. Electricity coursed through his veins and his heart twisted as all his blood coursed toward his groin. He looked down at her beautiful, shocked face, at her wide hazel eyes, at the way her pink lips parted, full and ripe for plunder.

Mouth parted, she jumped back as if he'd burned her.

"Give a girl some notice, will you," she snapped, "if you're just going to whip around like that!"

Her tone was scornful. But it was too late.

He knew.

For years, Vladimir had told himself that their passionate, innocent affair had all been one-sided—that she'd tricked him, creating a hunger and longing in him while she herself remained stone cold, focused only on the money she intended to steal from him. But just now, when he'd felt her body against his, he'd seen her face. Felt the way her body reacted. And he'd suddenly known the truth.

She felt it, too.

"You…you should…" Her voice faltered as their eyes locked. As they stood beside the four-poster bed, the brilliant sun burst over the horizon, coming through the tall east-facing windows, bathing them both in warm golden light. Everything he'd ever hungered for, everything he feared and despised, was personified in this one woman. *Breanna.*

Her long blond hair shimmered like diamonds and gold. Her eyes shone a vivid green, like emeralds. Her skin was pale and untouched, like plains of virgin white snow. Hardly aware of what he was doing, Vladimir reached out and stroked a gleaming tendril of her hair. It was impossibly soft.

He heard her soft intake of breath. "Please. Don't."

"Don't?" He looked into her eyes. "You want me," he said in a low voice. "Just as I want you."

Her luscious lips fell open. Then with a scowl, she shook her head fiercely. "You're out of your mind!"

"Don't you recognize the truth when you see it? Or have you forgotten how?"

"The only *truth* is I want you to leave me alone!"

Twining his fingers through her long blond hair, he pulled back, tilting her head to expose her throat.

"Whatever your words say," he whispered, "your lips won't lie."

And he ruthlessly lowered his mouth to hers.

His kiss was an overpowering force, savage enough to bruise. His grip was unyielding, like steel. Dree felt herself being crushed against his hard body.

Kiss? More like plunder. His lips were hard and rough. She felt his powerful hands on her back, felt their warmth through her leather jacket. The muscles of his hard chest crushed her breasts as he wrapped his arms tighter around her. He pushed her lips wider apart with his own, taking full possession of her mouth.

The tip of his tongue touched hers, and it was like two currents of electricity joining in a burst of light. Against her will, repressed desire exploded inside her, and need sizzled down her body like fire.

Her hands somehow stopped pushing against his chest, and lifted to wrap around his neck. It had been so long since she'd been touched by anyone, and he was the only man who'd ever kissed her. The only one she'd ever wanted. The man she'd loved with all her heart, the man who'd brought her to life and made her new.

Vladimir. As he kissed her, she sighed softly against his mouth. For ten long years, she'd dreamed of him every aching night. And now, at last, her dream was real. She was in his arms, he was kissing her....

But he'd never kissed her like this before. There was nothing loving about this embrace. It was scornful. Angry.

One of his legs pushed her thighs apart. His hands moved up to entwine his fingers in her hair, yanking her head back.

"No," she whimpered, feeling dizzy as she wrenched away. She put an unsteady hand to her forehead. "No."

Vladimir stared down at her. His gaze seemed almost bewildered. She heard the hard rasp of his breath, and realized that he, too, had been surprised. Then his face hardened.

"Why should I not kiss you?" He walked slowly around her, running one hand up her arm and the side of her neck. "You belong to me now, *kroshka*."

Kroshka? She didn't know what it meant, but it didn't sound very nice.

Stopping in front of her, he cupped her chin. He handled her carelessly, possessively, as a man might handle any valuable possession—a rifle, a jewel, a horse. Insolently, he traced his hand down her bare neck. "I intend to take full possession of my prize." His hand slid over her black T-shirt to the hollow between her breasts. "Soon you will be spread across my bed. Aching for me." His hand continued to slide down her waist. Gripping her hip, he suddenly pulled her hard against his body. "Your only reason to exist now is to serve me."

Shaking, she tried to toss her head. Tried to defy him. Instead, her voice trembled as she asked, "What are you going to do to me?"

"Whatever I please." He moved his hand up her body, cupping her breast over the T-shirt, tweaking her aching nipple with his thumb. As she gasped, he smiled. "But you will please me, Bree. Have no doubt about that."

She wanted to beg him to let her go. But she knew it would do no good. Vladimir's handsome, chiseled face was hard as granite. There was no mercy in it. But she couldn't stop herself from choking out, "Please don't do this."

"My touch wasn't always so distasteful to you," he said softly. He ran his hands down her shoulders, pulling off her black leather jacket and dropping it to the marble bedroom floor. "Once, you shuddered beneath me. You wanted me so badly you wept."

Bree swallowed. She'd once been sure of only two things on earth: that Vladimir Xendzov was the last honorable man in this selfish, cynical world. And that he loved her.

"Ya tebya lyublyu," he'd whispered. *I love you, Breanna. Be my wife. Be mine forever.*

He'd been a different man then, a man who laughed easily, who held her tenderly, a fellow orphan who looked at her with worship in his eyes. Now, his handsome face was a lifetime harder. He was a different man, hard and rough as an unpolished diamond, his blue gaze as cold as the place that had been his frequent home for the past ten years—Siberia.

His grip on her tightened as he said huskily, "Do you not remember?"

Blinking fast, she whispered, "That was when I loved you."

His hands grew still.

"You must think I'm a fool." Dropping his arms, he said coldly, "I know you never loved me. You loved my money, nothing more."

"It might have started as a con," she said tearfully, "but it changed to something more. I'm telling you the truth. I loved—"

"Say those words again," he exclaimed, cutting her off in a low, dangerous voice, "and you'll regret it."

She straightened her spine and looked at him defiantly.

"I loved you," she cried. "With all my heart!"

"Be quiet!" With a low growl, he pushed her back violently against the bedpost. "Not another word!"

Bree's heart pounded as she saw the fury in his eyes. She could feel the hard wood against her back, feel his chest against hers with the quick rise and fall of her every breath.

Abruptly, he released her.

"Why did you really come to Hawaii?" he said in a low voice.

She blinked fast, able to exhale. "We got offered jobs here, and we needed them."

He shook his head, his jaw tight. "Why would you take a job as a housekeeper? With your skills?" His eyes narrowed.

"You were surprised to see me at the poker table. If you're not here to con me, who was your mark?"

"No one! I told you—I don't do that anymore!"

"Right," he said sarcastically. "Because you're honest and pure."

His nasty tone cut her to the heart, but she raised her chin. "What are *you* doing here? Because the last time I checked, there weren't many gold mines on Oahu!"

He stared at her for a long moment. "Do you truly not know?" His forehead furrowed. "It was in the news…."

"I've spent the last decade *avoiding* news about you, chief. Not looking for it!"

"Three months ago, I was in an accident," he said tightly. "Racing on the Honolulu International Speedway."

An accident? As in—hurt?

She looked him over anxiously, but saw no sign of injury. Catching his eye, she scowled. "Too bad it didn't kill you."

"Yes. Too bad." His voice was cold. "I am fine now. I was planning to return to St. Petersburg tomorrow."

Her heart leaped with sudden hope. "So you're leaving—"

"I'm not in any hurry." He gripped her wrists again. "Nice try changing the subject. Tell me why you came here. Who is your mark? If not me, then who?"

"No one!"

"You expect me to believe we met by coincidence?"

She bared her teeth. "More like bad luck!"

"Bad luck," he muttered. He moved closer to her, and his grip tightened. She felt tingles down her body, felt his closeness as he pressed her against the carved wooden post of the bed. His gaze fell to her lips.

"No," she whispered. "Please." She swallowed, then lifted her gaze. "You said…I could just clean the house…."

He stared at her. His blue eyes were wide as the infinite blue sea. Then he abruptly let her go.

"As you wish," he said coldly. "On your back in my bed, or

breaking it scrubbing my floor—it makes little difference to me. Be downstairs in five minutes."

Turning on his heel, he left the bedroom. Bree's knees nearly collapsed, and she fell back against the bed.

Vladimir didn't believe she'd ever loved him. When he'd abandoned her to the sheriff that cold December night in Alaska, he'd truly believed that her love for him had just been an act. And now he was determined to exact revenge.

His punishing, soul-destroying kiss had been just the start. An appetizer. He intended to enjoy her humiliation like a lengthy gourmet meal, taking each exquisite course at his own leisure. He would feast on her pride, her body, her soul, her memories, her youth, her heart—until nothing was left but an empty shell.

With a silent sob, Bree dropped her face in her hands.

She was in real trouble.

CHAPTER FOUR

SEVEN hours later, Bree had never felt so sweaty and filthy in her life.

And she was glad.

With a sigh, she squeezed her sponge over the bucket of soapy water. There was still almost no dirt—she guessed Vladimir's team of servants had cleaned the place top to bottom the day before. But he'd still made her scrub every inch of the enormous house's marble floor. She narrowed her eyes. Tyrannical man. Her back ached, as did her arms and legs. But—and this was the part she was happy about—she'd done it all with her clothes on. He'd thought a little cleaning could humiliate her?

Leaning back on her haunches, Bree rubbed her cheek with her shoulder and smiled at the newly shining kitchen floor.

This house was a beautiful place, she'd give him that. Glancing through the windows as she'd worked all day, surreptitiously plotting her escape, she'd seen an Olympic-sized infinity pool clinging to the edge of the ocean cliff. On the other side of the house, across the tennis courts, she'd seen a cluster of small cottages on the edge of the compound, where she guessed Vladimir's invisible army of servants lived. Yes. She'd never seen such an amazing villa estate before.

But for all its luxury, it was still a prison. Just as, for all of Vladimir's dark, brooding good looks, he was her jailer.

She scowled, recalling how he'd enjoyed watching her on all fours, scrubbing his home office that morning. Her stomach had growled with hunger as Vladimir ate a lavish breakfast, served on a tray at his desk. The delicious smells of coffee and bacon had been torture to Bree, following a night where she'd had no food and barely two hours' sleep. His housekeeper, after watching with dismay, had disappeared. But Bree was proud of herself that she hadn't given Vladimir the satisfaction of seeing her whimper.

No more whimpering, she vowed.

Bree jumped as Vladimir suddenly stalked into the kitchen, his posture angry. He stomped into the room and opened one of the doors of the big refrigerator.

Biting her lip, she looked away, scrubbing the floor harder with her sponge. But he was making so much noise, she glanced at him out of the corner of her eye.

He grabbed homemade bread from the cupboard and ripped off a hunk. Tossing it onto a plate, he chopped through it with a big knife, like a grim executioner with an ax. She gulped, watching in bewilderment as he added cheese, chicken, even mustard and tomato. He opened the fridge and added a bottle of water and then a linen napkin to the tray. His Italian leather shoes were heavy against the marble floor as he came over to her, holding out the tray with a glower.

"Your lunch," he said coldly.

Her belly rumbled in response. She'd had nothing to eat since a cheerless Christmas dinner yesterday, a bologna sandwich eaten alone at the end of her housekeeping shift. Sitting back on her haunches, Bree wiped her sweaty forehead and looked up at him.

Unlike her, Vladimir had taken a shower, and looked sleek, urbane and civilized in a freshly pressed black button-down shirt and black trousers. His tanned skin glowed with health, smelling faintly of soap and sandalwood.

While she...

She wasn't feeling so pretty. She'd peeled off her boots to work barefoot on the wet floor. Her long blond hair was twisted into a messy knot at the back of her head, to lift it off her hot neck. Her T-shirt was sweaty all the way through, and in the humidity of Hawaii, even with air-conditioning she knew she looked like a swamp creature from a 1950s horror movie.

She narrowed her eyes. If he thought she was going to lick his boots with gratitude for the simple courtesy of lunch, he had another think coming. His *serf!*

She looked at the tray. He waited.

"I don't like tomatoes," she said pleasantly.

Vladimir dropped the tray with a noisy clatter on the floor beside her. "Tough. I have no desire to cater to you, and Mrs. Kalani decided to take the rest of the day off."

Bree looked up at him, and a slow grin lifted her cheeks. "She gave you a hard time about me, didn't she?"

"Enjoy your lunch." He pointed to an immaculate section of the floor. "You missed a spot."

Vladimir had thrown the tray down as if she were the family golden retriever. Rising to her feet after he left, she washed her hands, then took the tray to the dining table like a civilized person, ready for a fight if he came back to give her one. Somewhat to her disappointment, he didn't.

Once she'd removed the tomatoes, the freshly baked bread made the rest of the sandwich delicious. Honey mustard was a nice touch, too. And the cold, sparkling water was just what she'd wanted. She wiped her mouth.

He was still a brute. Her eyes narrowed as she remembered his cold words.

For the rest of your life, you will work for me, Bree. For free. You will never be paid, or allowed to leave. Your only goal, until you die, is to serve me and give me pleasure.

He didn't know who he was dealing with. She finished off the cold water and tidied up the tray. He thought a little housecleaning would kill her? She'd been training for this for the past ten years.

She was going to escape this captivity. As soon as she could formulate a plan.

As the afternoon wore on, Bree scrubbed her way fiercely up the stairs and then cleaned five guest bedrooms, which had already been as sparkling clean as the rest of the house. But as she reached the master bedroom, the sun was starting to lower in the western sky, and her whole body ached. She couldn't stop yawning. Looking at the four-poster bed, she was tempted to take a short power nap. Vladimir would never know, she told herself. Climbing onto the large, soft bed, she closed her eyes—just for a few minutes.

With a gasp, Bree sat up suddenly in bed. The room was now dark. She looked over at the clock. It was almost seven o'clock. Dinnertime.

She'd slept for hours.

Feeling sweaty and gross, her body aching, Bree rose stiffly from the still-made bed, stretching her arms over her head. She rubbed her eyes with her knuckles. So where was her slave driver? Why hadn't he discovered her napping? Tsar Vladimir the Terrible must be hard at work, she decided, planning a new way to humiliate her, or dreaming up some nefarious new attack on his brother. When she'd been cleaning his home office, he'd been talking rather intensely in Russian on the phone. But even then, his smoldering gaze had slowly wandered over her backside as she scrubbed the floors on all fours.

Fine. Let him look.

With a deep breath, Bree closed her eyes. As long as he didn't touch. As long as she didn't have to feel his lips, hot and hard against her own, as he held her so tightly against his body…

"You're awake."

At the sound of Vladimir's husky voice from the doorway, she jumped, whirling around. "You—you knew I was sleeping?" she stammered.

His gaze was intense as he came toward her. "Yes."

She felt suddenly very small as his tall body loomed over hers. She licked her lips. "So why didn't you wake me up and start bossing me around?"

Reaching out, he brushed a tendril of hair out of her eyes. "Because you looked like an angel."

His voice was low. Sensual. Bree's eyes widened as she looked up—no, not at his lips! His *eyes!* Trembling with awareness at how they were once again alone in his bedroom, she tightened her hands at her sides. "Um. Thanks. For letting me borrow your bed." She edged away from it. "I should probably be getting back to work...."

His eyes glimmered. "*Our* bed."

"What?"

Vladimir's large hand wrapped around the post's polished wood. "You called it my bed. It is ours."

Her lips parted. Then she folded her arms protectively against her chest. "Look. Whatever our wager was, you can't actually expect me to..."

"Expect you to what?"

"Sleep with you."

"You were serious when you offered it as a prize." He looked down at her. "'My skills at cards are nothing compared to what I can do to you in bed,' you said." His tone was mocking. "'A single hour with me will change your whole life,' you said!"

Shivering, she looked away. "I was bluffing," she said in a small voice. "I don't know how to do those things." Her cheeks colored, and shame burned through her as she looked at the marble floor. "I've never been with a man before. I've never even kissed a man—since..." She bit her lip and muttered, "Not since you."

He stared at her. "You're a *virgin?*"

His voice dripped disbelief. A lump rose to her throat, and she nodded.

"Right," he said scornfully. "You're a virgin."

She lifted her head in outrage. "You think I'm a liar?"

"I know you are." His cool blue eyes met hers. "You lie about everything. You can't help it. Lying is in your blood."

Lying is in your blood. Before Bree's mother died, her parents had been regular law-abiding citizens, childhood sweethearts married at eighteen, high school teachers who mowed the lawn in Alaska's short, bright summers and shoveled snow through eight-month winters. Her mother had taught English, her father science. Then, at thirty, Lois Dalton had contracted cancer. Newly pregnant with her second child, she'd put off chemo treatments that might risk her baby. Two months after Josie's birth, Lois had died. Jack Dalton lost his wife, his best friend and, some said, his mind....

He'd quit his job as a teacher. He left the new baby with a sitter. And every day, after he picked up Bree from first grade, he took her to backroom poker games. First in Anchorage, and then to ports where Alaskan cruises deposited new tourists each day. With each success, his plans had grown more daring. And they'd worked. At first.

Pushing the memory aside, Bree shook her head. "I'm not lying. I'm a virgin!"

"Stop it. You made the bet. You made your bed." Vladimir lightly trailed his hand above her head, along the carved wooden post. "Now you will sleep in it."

She glared at him, setting her jaw. "I only made that bet because I was desperate—because I had nothing else remotely valuable to offer! For Josie—"

"Josie was safe. You had more than enough."

A sudden thought struck Bree, and she caught her breath. "Did you...let me win?" she whispered. "Is that why you kept raising the stakes—why you egged me on during the game? So that I could cover Josie's debt?"

His jaw tightened. "I thought she was some innocent kid that Hudson had lured into the game. Not like you." His eyes flashed as he looked down at Bree. "You could have walked away. But when I offered you the one-card gamble, you accepted. There was no desperation. It was pure greed. And it told me what I needed to know."

She swallowed. "What?"

"That you hadn't changed. You were still using your body as bait."

She took a deep breath and whispered, "I never thought in a million years that I would lose that game." Exhaustion suddenly swamped her like a wave. Tears rose to her eyes. "And if you were any kind of decent man, you would never expect me to actually…"

"To what? Follow through on your promise?" He gave a hard laugh. "No, what kind of monster would expect that?"

Bree exhaled. "How stupid can I be, appealing to your better nature?"

"I won. You lost." He folded his arms, staring at her with his eyes narrowed. "You have many, many faults, Bree Dalton. Almost too many to count. In fact, your faults are like grains of sand on a beach that stretches across the whole wide world…"

"All right, I get it," she muttered. "You don't exactly admire me."

"…but I never thought," he continued, his eyes glinting, "that you'd be a sore loser."

Bree stared up at him mutinously. Then, setting her jaw, she turned away and stomped over to the bucket of cold water. She snatched up the scraggly sponge and held it up like a sword.

"Fine," she snapped. "What do you want me to scrub? The bottom of your Lamborghini? The concrete around the pool? A patch of mud by the garden? I don't even care. But we both know your house is already *clean!*"

His sensual mouth curved at the edges. Gently, he took the sponge out of her hand and dropped it with a soft splash into the bucket. "You can stop cleaning anytime you want."

She searched his eyes. "I can?"

He put his hands on her shoulders, looking down at her.

"Come to bed with me," he said quietly.

Flashes of heat went up and down her body. His hands on her shoulders were heavy, sensual, like points of light. With an intake of breath, she ripped herself away from him.

"Dream on," she said, tossing her head with every ounce of bravado she possessed.

He shrugged. "Then I'll have to find some other way to make you useful."

Bree started to reach for the bucket and sponge, but he stopped her. "No. You are right. Enough cleaning." He gave a sudden wicked grin. "You will cook for me."

Her jaw dropped. He must have forgotten the last time she'd cooked for him, taking a romantic date idea from a magazine. It had been romantic, all right—she'd nearly burned the cabin down, and then the firemen had been called. "You can't be serious."

Vladimir lifted a dark eyebrow. "Because you're still a terrible cook?"

She glared at him. "Because you know I would poison you!"

"I know you won't, because we will share the meal." He leaned forward and said softly, "Tonight I am craving…something delicious." She saw the edge of his tongue flick the corner of his sensual lips. "Something sinful."

Even though he was talking about food, his low voice caused a shiver of awareness down her spine. She swallowed.

"Well, were you thinking chicken noodle soup from a can?" she suggested weakly. "Because I know how to make that."

"Tempting. But no." He tilted his head. "A goat cheese soufflé with Provençal herbs."

Her mouth dropped. "Are you kidding?"

"Try it." His lips turned up at the corners. "You might like it."

"I might like to eat it, but I can't cook it!"

"If you cook it, I will allow you to have some."

"Generous of you."

"Of course." Innocently, he spread his arms wide. "What am I, some kind of heartless brute?"

"You really want me to answer that?"

He gave a low, wicked laugh. "It's a beautiful night. You will come out onto the lanai and cook for me."

"Fine." She looked at him dubiously. "It's your funeral."

And so half an hour later, Bree found herself on the patio beside the pool, in the sheltered outdoor kitchen, struggling to sauté garlic and flour in garlic oil.

"This recipe is ridiculous!" She sneezed violently as minced thyme sprinkled the air like snowflakes, instead of coating the melted butter in the soufflé pan. "It's meant for four cooks and a sous-chef, not one person!"

Vladimir, who sat at the large granite table with an amazing view of the sunset-swept Pacific beyond the infinity pool, sipped an extremely expensive wine as he read a Russian newspaper. "You're exaggerating. For a clever woman like you, surely arranging a few herbs and whipping up a few eggs is not so difficult. How hard can it be to chop and sauté?"

She waved her knife at him furiously. "Come a little closer and I'll show you!"

"Stop complaining," he said coldly, taking another sip of merlot.

"Oh," Bree gasped, realizing she was supposed to be whisking flour and garlic in the hot olive oil. She tried to focus, not wanting to let Vladimir break her, but cooking had never been her skill. Supervising a kitchen staff? No problem. Cracking the eggs herself? A huge mess. She suddenly smelled burning oil, and remembered she was supposed to keep stirring the milk and white wine in the pan until it boiled. As she rushed across the outdoor kitchen, her bare feet slid on an egg white she'd spilled earlier. She skidded, then slipped, and as her tailbone slammed against the tile floor, the whisked egg yolks in her bowl flew up in the air before landing, wet and sticky, in her hair.

Suddenly, Vladimir was kneeling beside her. "Are you hurt, Breanna?"

She stared at him. She felt his powerful arms around her, protective and strong, as he lifted her to her feet.

Trembling, Bree stared up at him, wide-eyed. "You called me Breanna."

He stiffened. Abruptly, he released her.

"It is your name," he said coldly.

Without his arms encircling her, she felt suddenly cold and shivery and—alone. For a moment she'd seen an emotion flicker in his eyes that had made her wonder if he…

No. She'd been wrong. He didn't care about her. Whatever feelings he'd once had for her had disappeared at the first sign of trouble.

Right?

Bree had certainly never intended to love him. The night they'd met, she'd known him only as the young CEO of a start-up mining company, whose family had once owned the land her father had bought in trust for Josie a few years before. "Promise me," Black Jack had wheezed from the hospital bed, before he died. "Promise me you'll always take care of your sister."

In her desperation to be free and keep Josie safe, Bree had known she'd do anything to get the money she needed. And the best way to make Vladimir Xendzov careless about his money was to make him care about her. To dazzle him.

But from the moment they'd met, Bree had been the one who was dazzled. She'd never met a man like Vladimir: so honest, so open, so protective. For the first time in her life, she'd seen the possibilities of a future beyond the next poker game. She'd seen she could be something more than a cheap con artist with a rusted heart. He'd called her by her full name, Breanna, and made her feel brand-new. *I love you, Breanna. Be my wife. Be mine forever.*

Now she blinked, staring up at him in the deepening twilight. Vladimir was practically scowling at her, his arms folded, his blue eyes dark.

But the way he'd said her name when he'd held her… His voice had sounded the same as ten years ago. Exactly the same.

Vladimir growled a low Russian curse. "You're a mess. Go take a shower. Wash the food out of your hair. Get clean clothes." He snatched the empty saucepan from her hand. "Just go. I will finish this."

Now, that was truly astonishing. "You—you will cook?"

"You are even more helpless in the kitchen than I remembered," he said harshly. "Go. I left new clothes for you in the bedroom upstairs. Get cleaned up. Return in a more presentable state."

Bree's lips were parted as she stared at him. He was actually being nice to her. No matter how harsh his tone, or how he couched his kindness inside insults, there could be no doubt. He was allowing her to take a shower, to change into clean clothes, like a guest. Not a slave.

Why? What could he possibly gain by kindness, when he held all the power? "Thank you." She swallowed. "I really appreciate—"

"Save it." He cut her off. Setting down the pan on the granite island of the outdoor kitchen, he looked at her. "At least until you see the dress I've left on your bed. Take a shower and put it on. Afterwards, come back here." He gave her a hard, sensual smile. "And then…then you can thank me."

Vladimir should have known not to make her cook.

He'd thought that Bree, at age twenty-eight, might have improved her skills. No. If possible, she'd grown even more hopeless in the kitchen. The attempt had been a complete disaster, even before the raw yolks had been flung all over—perhaps a merciful end before they could be added to the burned, lumpy mess in the sauté pan.

Cleaning up, he dumped it all out and started fresh. Forty

minutes later, he sat at the table on the patio and tasted his finished soufflé, and gave a satisfied sigh.

He would not ask Bree to make food again.

Vladimir knew how to cook. He just preferred not to. When he was growing up, his family had had nothing. His father tried his best to keep up the six-hundred-acre homestead, but he'd had his head in the clouds—the kind of man who would be mulling over a book of Russian philosophy and not notice that their newborn calf had just wandered away from its mother to die in a snowdrift. Vladimir's mother, a former waitress from the Lower Forty-Eight, had been a little in awe of her intellectual husband, with his royal background. Her days were spent cleaning up the messes her absentminded spouse left behind, to make sure they had enough wood to get through the winter, and food for their two growing boys. It was because of their father's influence that Vladimir and Kasimir had both applied to one of the oldest mining schools in Europe, in St. Petersburg. It was because of their mother's influence they'd managed to pay for it, but in a way that had broken her husband's heart. And that was nothing compared to how Vladimir had found the money to start Xendzov Mining OAO twelve years ago. That had been the spark that started the brothers' war. That had caused Kasimir to turn on him so viciously.

Vladimir's eyes narrowed. His brother deserved what he'd gotten—being cut out of the company right before it would have made him insanely rich. He, Vladimir, had deserved to own the company free and clear.

Just as he owned Bree Dalton.

He had a sudden memory of her stricken hazel eyes, of her pale, beautiful face.

You called me Breanna.

Rising from his chair, Vladimir paced three steps across the patio. He stopped, staring at the moonlight sparkling across the pool and the ocean beyond.

She really must think he was a fool. She must have no respect whatsoever for his intelligence, to think that she could look at him with those beautiful luminous eyes and make him believe she'd actually loved him once. It would not work. They both knew it had always been about money for her. It still was.

I've never been with a man before. I've never even kissed a man since you.

Reaching for his wine glass, he took a long drink and then wiped his mouth. She was a fairly good liar, he'd give her that. But he was immune to her now. Absolutely immune.

Except for her body.

He'd enjoyed watching her scrub his floors, watching the sway of slender hips, of her backside and breasts as she knelt in front of him. He'd wanted to take her, then and there.

And he would. Soon.

Their kiss had been electric. He still shuddered to remember the softness of her body as she'd clung to him. The scent of her, like orchids and honey. The sweet, erotic taste of her lips. He'd intended to punish her with that savage kiss. Instead, he'd been lost in it, in memory, in yearning, in hot ruthless need.

Gritting his teeth, he roughly tidied up the outdoor kitchen, slamming the dirty pans into the sink. No matter how he tried to deny it, Bree still had power over him. Too much. When he'd seen her slip and fall on this floor, her cry had sliced straight through his heart. And suddenly, without knowing how, he'd found himself beside her, helping her to her feet.

You called me Breanna.

Irritated, he exhaled, setting his jaw. He glanced up toward the house. It had been almost an hour. What was taking her so long?

He grabbed a plate and served her a portion of the soufflé, then took a crystal goblet from the cupboard on the lanai. He carried them both over to the tray on the granite table, beside the open bottle of merlot. He looked out at the shimmering pool, at the crashing waves of the dark ocean below the cliff. He tried to relax his shoulders, to take a deep breath.

After he'd nearly died in the car crash on the raceway, his doctor had arrived from St. Petersburg and told him he needed to find a less risky way to relax. "You're thirty-five years old, Your Highness," the doctor had said gravely. "But you have the blood pressure of a much older man. You're a heart attack waiting to happen." So Vladimir, wrapped up in bandages over his broken bones, had grimly promised to give up car racing forever, along with boxing and skydiving. He'd bought this house and started physical rehabilitation. He'd done yoga and tai chi.

Or at least he'd tried.

He hadn't made it through a single yoga class. The more he tried to calm down, the more he felt the vein in his neck throb until his forehead was covered with sweat. The pain of doing nothing, of just sitting alone with his thoughts, left him half-mad, like a tiger trapped in a cage.

He'd done extreme sports because they made him feel something. The adrenaline stirred up by thinking he might die was a reminder that he was still alive. The never ending sameness of his work, of one meaningless love affair after another, sometimes made him forget.

And *yoga* was supposed to relax him? Vladimir grumbled beneath his breath. Stupid doctors. What did they know?

He'd already had twelve weeks of twiddling his thumbs, "healing" as ordered, while knowing his brother was in Morocco, tying up various gold and diamond sources in underhanded ways. When his leg had healed enough for him to drive, Vladimir had bought the new Lamborghini to go to the weekly private poker game at the Hale Ka'nani Resort. Then he'd found Bree, who drove him absolutely insane. Even more than yoga.

But what the hell was taking her so long? The dinner he'd made was growing cold. Scowling, he looked up at the second-floor bedroom balcony. How long could it take for a woman to shower?

"Bree," he yelled. "Come down."

"No," he heard her yell back from the open French doors of the balcony.

He set his jaw. "Right now!"

"Forget it! I'm not wearing this thing!"

"Then you won't eat!"

"Fine by me!"

This dinner wasn't going at all as he'd envisioned. Growling to himself, Vladimir left the dinner tray on the table and raced inside. Taking the stairs two at a time, he went down the hall and shoved open the double doors to the master bedroom, knocking them back against the walls.

Bree whirled around with a gasp.

Vladimir took one look and his mouth went slack. His heart nearly stopped in his chest.

She stood half-naked, wearing the expensive lingerie, a pale pink teddy and silk robe he'd had a servant buy for her in Kailua. "Make it tacky," Vladimir had instructed. "The sort of thing a stripper might wear."

He'd meant to humiliate her. In spite of Bree's corrupt, hollow soul, she'd always dressed modestly. She never showed any skin—ever. Even when she'd done her best to entice the men at the poker game, she'd lured them with her words, with her electrifying voice, with her angelic face and slender body. But she'd been completely covered from head to toe, with jeans and a leather jacket.

Vladimir had never seen this much of her bare skin. Not even the night ten years ago when he'd proposed, when they would have made love if they hadn't been interrupted. The lingerie should have looked slutty. It didn't.

The pale pink color reflected the blush on her cheeks. She looked innocent and young. Like a bride on her wedding night.

Anger and frustration rushed through him. Each time he tried to humiliate Bree or teach her a lesson, she stymied him.

Furious, he crossed the bedroom. Reaching out his hand, he heard her intake of breath as he ripped off the short silken robe, dropping it to the floor. His eyes raked over the creamy skin of her bare shoulders. The slip of silk beneath barely reached the tops of her thighs, and the flimsy bodice revealed most of the curves of her breasts. He saw the thrust of her nipples through the silk, and was instantly hard.

Bree's cheeks burned red as she glared at him. "Are you happy?"

"No," he growled. He roughly pulled her into his arms. "But I will be."

Her eyes glittered. "So you won me in a poker game. Is this what you wanted, Vladimir? To make me look like your whore?"

He saw the shimmer in her eyes, the vulnerability on her beautiful face, heard the heart-stopping tremble of her voice, and felt that same strange twist in his chest. *It's nothing more than an act to manipulate me,* he told himself fiercely. Damn her!

"You sold yourself to me of your own free will," he growled. "What other word would you use to describe a woman who does such a thing?"

He heard the furious intake of her breath, saw the rapid rise and fall of her chest. But as she drew her hand back to slap him, he caught her wrist.

"Typical feminine reaction," he observed coldly. "I expected more of you."

"How about this," she hissed, ripping her arm away. Her damp blond hair slid against the bare skin of her shoulders. *"I hate you."*

His lips curled. "Good."

"I wish to God we'd never met. That any man but you had won me." Her eyes flashed fire. "I'd rather be right now in the bed of any man at the table—"

Her voice ended with a choke as he yanked her against his body. "So you admit, then, that you are exactly as I've said. A liar, a cheat and a whore."

Her beautiful hazel eyes widened beneath the dark fringe of lashes. Then she swallowed and looked down. "I was a liar, yes, and a cheat, too, but never—never the other," she said in a small voice. She shook her head. "I haven't tried to con anyone for ten years. You changed me." Her dark lashes rose. "You made me a better person," she whispered. The pain and bewilderment in her eyes made her seem suddenly young and fragile and sad. "And you left."

And he felt it again—the tight twist in the place where his heart should have been. As if he were an ogre standing over a poor peasant girl with a whip.

No! Damn it! He wouldn't feel sorry for her!

He'd show her that her overt display of a wobbly lower lip and big hazel eyes had no effect on him whatsoever!

Bree Dalton didn't have feelings, he told himself fiercely. Just masks. He glared at her. "Stop it."

"What?"

"Your ridiculous attempt to gain my sympathy. It—"

It won't work, he meant to say, but his throat closed as he was distracted by the rise and fall of her breasts in the tiny slip of blush-colored silk when she breathed. He could see the shape of her nipples and the way they trembled with every hard breath.

And he was rock hard. Their mutual dislike somehow only made him desire her more, to almost unsustainable need. What magnetic control did she have over his body? Why did he want her like this? She was a confessed liar, a con artist. She wished she'd lost her body to any man but him. How could he want her still? It was almost as if she wasn't his slave at all, but he was hers.

And that enraged him most of all.

A low growl came from the back of his throat. He was in control. Not her.

His hands tightened into fists, his jaw clenching. He wanted to push Bree against the bed, to kiss her hard, to plunge himself inside her and make her scream with pleasure. He wanted to make her explode with pure ecstasy, even while she hated him. A grim smile curved his lips. She would despise herself for that, which would be sweet indeed.

But when he took her, it would be in his own time. At his free choice. Not because she'd driven him to madness by her taunts and the seductive sway of her nubile body.

He wouldn't let her conquer him.

His shoulders ached with tension as he turned away, fighting for self-control. He looked around the master bedroom with a derisive curl on his lip. "I can see you did not finish scrubbing this floor before you took your long lazy nap. You will finish it now. While I watch."

Her expression changed. Snatching up the frayed sponge, she grabbed the bucket of cold wash water from the floor and, in a posture of clear fury, knelt down. He watched her slender, delectable body, wearing only the tiny slip of pink silk, moving back and forth on all fours as she scrubbed the floor. His mouth went dry.

Bree looked up.

"Enjoying the show?" she said coldly.

Without a word, Vladimir turned and left the bedroom. He returned a moment later with his own dinner tray and red wine. Still not speaking, he sat down in a cushioned chair near the marble fireplace. Calmly he unfolded his fine linen napkin across his lap.

"Now I am," he replied.

Sitting back comfortably in his chair, he took a sip of merlot. He had the satisfaction of seeing her eyes widen, of seeing her scowl. Then she turned back to her work, and he had the even greater satisfaction of watching Bree on all fours, her body frosted with silvery moonlight, scrubbing his floor with a sponge and a pail of water.

Outside the veranda window, the full moon lit up the shimmering dark Pacific. The large master bedroom was full of shadows, lit only by a single lamp near his massive four-poster bed. With the flick of a remote, Vladimir turned on the gas fireplace, adding soft flickering firelight to better see his dinner—and the floor show. His solid silver knife and fork slid noisily against the pure bone china, edged with 24 karat gold, as he cut the Provençal goat cheese and Gruyère soufflé. Watching her, he took a bite.

It was exquisite. He sighed in true, deep pleasure.

"Tasty?" Bree muttered, not looking at him.

"You have no idea." His homemade soufflé was indeed delicious, but he wasn't referring to the food.

"I hope you choke and die," she said sweetly.

"Don't forget the area by the bed." He watched Bree's nearly naked body shimmy as she scrubbed. His eyes ran along her slender, toned legs, the sweet curve of her backside, her plump breasts hanging down as they swayed, barely covered by the whisper-thin silk hanging from her shoulders.

Hmm. He didn't want to enjoy it *this* much. He shifted uncomfortably in his seat, moving his plate closer to his knees.

"Of course, *Your Highness.*" Giving him an *I-wish-you-were-dead* glare, Bree stomped—if a woman could be said to stomp while she was crawling—over to the foot of the bed, dragging the bucket behind her. It changed her body's position, giving Vladimir an entirely different view.

He was now sitting directly behind her. All he needed to do was get down on his knees, grab her hips in his hands and pull her sweet bottom back against his groin. It was suddenly all he could think about.

You're in control, he ordered himself. *Not her.*

But his body wasn't listening. A bead of sweat formed on his forehead. His hands clenched on the silver tray in his lap. Well, why not just take her? Bree was his property. His serf. His slave. She'd sold herself to him freely, taunting him with her sexual skill. *You have no idea what I can do to you.* An untouched virgin—Bree? Impossible. She was an experienced seductress. He'd wanted her. Waited for her. For ten years. So what was stopping him?

Vladimir watched the bounce of her breasts and slow up-and-down motion of her hips as she scrubbed the floor angrily.

Not a damned thing.

He heard a loud crash of breaking china. He'd risen to his feet without even knowing it. The tray had fallen from his lap, and his dinner was now a mess of broken crockery.

At the noise, Bree leaned back on her haunches, brushing a tendril of hair out of her face with her shoulder. Turning her luscious body in the tiny, clinging silk teddy, she glared at him. "I'm not cleaning that."

Then she saw the look in his eyes. Twisting away with an intake of breath, she started to scrub the floor again. This time with enough panicked force to dig right through the marble to the house's foundation and straight through the earth to Russia.

He stepped over the broken china. He stopped behind her. He fell to his knees.

"I'm not done," she choked out.

Wrapping his body around her back, he reached in front of her. He put his larger hand over hers, forcing the sponge to be still. His hand tightened as she tried, without success, to keep scrubbing. Caught between two opposing forces, the sponge ripped apart.

Bewildered, she leaned back with half a sponge in her hand. "Look what you did," she said, blinking fast. "You destroyed it. After everything it tried to do for you…"

"Bree," he said in a low voice.

Dropping the sponge, she closed her eyes, wrapping her arms around her shivering body. "Don't…"

But he was ruthless. Grabbing her hips with both hands, he pulled her body back against his own. He felt the rapid, panicked rise and fall of her ribs beneath the chain of his arms. Felt the sweet softness of her backside pressing into his hard, aching groin.

Slowly she opened her eyes and twisted her head to glance at him. Her skin was flushed, her cheeks pink. Her lips parted. He saw the nervous flicker of her tongue against the corner of her mouth.

And he could bear it no longer.

Roughly turning her in his arms, he pulled her to face him, body to body. Twining his hands in her tangled hair, he savagely lowered his mouth to hers.

For an instant, she stiffened. Then, with a little anguished cry, her lips melted against his own. She wrapped her arms around him, and in a rush, their grip tightened as they embraced in the devouring passion of a decade's hunger.

CHAPTER FIVE

BREE had to push him away. She should. She *must*.

She couldn't.

His kiss was hard, even angry—passionate, yes, but nothing like the tender way he'd once embraced her. His chin was rough with five-o'clock shadow, and his powerful arms held her tightly against him as they knelt facing each other, bodies pressed together. Even through his black trousers, she could feel how much he wanted her. And she wanted him.

You are my serf, he'd informed her coldly. *Your only reason for living, until you die, is to serve me and give me pleasure.* She'd been enraged. She was no man's slave.

But he wasn't taking her by force, as her lord and master. No—she couldn't kid herself about that. Because no matter how badly he treated her, she still wanted him. She'd never stopped wanting him....

Vladimir's body moved as he took full, hard possession of her lips, stretching her mouth wide with his own, teasing her with his tongue. His hands moved against her back, sliding the thin, blush-colored silk teddy like a whisper against her naked skin. Her breasts felt heavy and taut, her nipples sizzling with awareness.

As he slowly kissed down her neck, her head fell backward. Breathless with need, she closed her eyes. His tongue flicked her collarbone, his hands cupping her breasts through the silk.

"Breanna," he whispered. "You feel so good. Just like I dreamed you would…"

His breath was warm against her skin as he lowered his head to suckle her through the silk.

She gasped. The sensation of his hot wet mouth against her hard, aching nipple flooded her nerve endings with pleasure. Her fingertips dug into his shoulders as her toes curled beneath her. She pulled him closer.

He sucked gently through the silk, and she felt the fabric move softly, caressing her skin. With agonizing slowness, he pulled the bodice down, and cupped her naked breasts. She felt the roughness of his palm as he rubbed her, then pinched her taut nipples, presenting first one, then the other, to the wet, welcoming warmth of his mouth. Lost in sweet pleasure, she held her breath….

She almost wept in frustration when he suddenly pulled away from her, leaving her bereft. Rising to his feet, he picked her up off the floor as if she weighed nothing at all. He carried her three steps to the bed, then tossed her on the white bedspread.

Eyes wide, Bree leaned back against the pillows and watched as Vladimir stood beside the bed, unbuttoning his shirt. His gaze locked with hers as he undid the cuffs and tossed the shirt to the floor. She had a brief vision of his tanned, muscled chest laced with dark hair before he fell on top of her, pulling her to him for a hard, hungry kiss.

It wasn't gentle or kind. It was primal, filled with fury at his unwilling need. She felt the heavy weight of his muscular body as he pushed her against the mattress. And as he kissed her, the world seemed to spin in a blinding flash of light. She kissed him back fiercely, desperately, forgetting pride and past pain beneath the overwhelming demand of desire.

Without a word, he ripped the pale pink silk teddy off her unresisting body. He looked down at her, now dressed only in the silk G-string panties he'd given her.

"I wanted you to learn your place." His voice was low, almost choked. Reaching out, he stroked her bare breasts in wonder, even as his other hand stroked up and down the length of her nearly naked body. "Instead you teach me mine." His dark blue eyes lifted to hers. "Why do you not touch me? Why do you hold back?"

She remembered her bravado at the poker table, the way she'd bragged about her skills in bed. Her cheeks flooded with heat. "I want to," she whispered. "I don't know how."

"You—don't know how?" he said in disbelief.

"I…" She swallowed. "I might have implied more than my skills actually deserve. At the poker table…"

"I don't give a damn about the game." He gripped her hand. "Just touch me. If you want to please me, touch me. If you want to punish me," he groaned, guiding her palm to stroke slowly down his chest to his belly, "touch me."

Vladimir truly had no idea that she was a virgin. Her fingers shook as she let him guide her, stroking his hard muscles, his hot, bare skin. She'd told him, but he hadn't believed her.

Suddenly, she didn't want him to know. Because how would he react if he learned the pathetic truth—that even after he'd abandoned her, she'd never wanted another man to touch her? Would his eyes fill with scorn—or pity?

She shuddered. He must never realize how much of a fool she'd been, or how thoroughly he'd destroyed her ten years ago.

She had to fake it.

Pretend to be the experienced woman he believed her to be.

So how would a sexually adventurous woman behave?

Trembling, Bree reached for his shoulders. Tossing her head with bravado, she rolled him beneath her on the bed. He did not resist, just looked up at her with smoldering eyes dark with lust. Trying to seem as if she was comfortable straddling him, with her breasts naked for a man for the first time, and wearing nothing but the tiny silk G-string, she gazed down at him. He did have an incredible body…and as long as she didn't look directly into his deep blue eyes, those eyes that always saw straight through her...

With an intake of breath, she slowly stroked down his bare chest to the waistband of his black trousers. Shaking with nerves, trying to act confident, she lowered her head.

And she kissed him.

Her lips were tentative, scared. Until she felt his mouth, hot and hard against hers, sliding like liquid silk as he kissed her back. He deepened the embrace, entwining her tongue with his. He tasted like sweet wine and spice and everything forbidden, everything she'd ever denied herself. His lips were soft and hard at once, like satin with steel. He let her set the rhythm and pace, let her lead.

And she forgot her fear. Her hands explored the warm, smooth skin of his hard chest, the edges and curves of his muscles. She stroked his flat nipples and the rough, bristly hair that stretched down his taut torso like an arrow. She heard his ragged intake of breath, and when she glanced up and saw his mesmerized expression, her confidence leaped. It was working! Growing bolder, she ran her fingertips beneath the edge of his waistband, swaying her splayed body against the thick hardness between his legs.

She'd meant it as an exploration. He took it as a taunt. With a growl, he pushed her back against the bed. Pulling off his pants and boxers, he kicked them to the floor.

She gasped when she saw him naked for the first time. He was huge. She couldn't look away. But as he pulled her back into his arms, crushing her breasts against his chest as he took possession of her mouth with a hard, hungry kiss, she forgot that fear, too.

He kissed slowly down her body, moving from her neck to the valley between her breasts to the flat plain of her belly. His hot breath enflamed her skin. Pushing her legs apart with his hands, he nuzzled her tender, untouched thighs. He kissed the edges of her G-string panties, and she felt the brief flicker of his tongue through silk.

She gasped. Need pounded through her, making her body shake as she felt his mouth move between her legs, gently suckling secret places there. She felt the heat and dampness of his tongue, teasing her on the edge of the fabric, and her back arched against the mattress. With a little cry, she stretched out her arms to grip the sheets, feeling as if she might fly off the bed and into the sky.

His fingers stroked the smooth silk, and she heard the rasp of her own frantic breathing. With tantalizing slowness, he reached beneath the fabric, stroking her wet core with a feather-like touch. He pushed a single thick fingertip an inch inside her, bending his head to suckle the top of her mound through the silk panties, and her back arched higher, her body grew tighter, and her breathing quickened, so much she started to see stars.

She heard the ripping of fabric as he destroyed the wisp of silk and tossed it to the floor.

"Look at me."

Against her will, she opened her eyes. Holding her gaze, he lowered his head between her naked thighs and fully tasted her with his wide tongue.

She cried out as she felt him tantalize, then lick, then lap her wet core. Her body twisted with the intensity of the pleasure even as her soul was torn by the intimacy of his gaze. Her heart hammered in her throat. Closing her eyes, she turned away so he could not see her tears.

His tongue changed rhythm; now he was using just the tip on her taut, sensitive nub. It was perfect. It was torture. His tongue swirled in light circles, barely touching her. She ached deep inside, wanting to be filled, wanting to have him inside her. Pleasure was building so hard and fast that her body could barely contain it. She felt an agony of need. With a whimper, she tried to pull away, but he held her firmly, not allowing her to escape from his hot, wet tongue.

Pleasure built higher and higher. "Please," she panted, nearly crying with need. "Please."

Holding her down, Vladimir thrust two thick fingertips inside her, then three. Still lapping her, he stretched her wide, his free hand pushing her back against the bed, while his tongue tormented her wet, slick core. And suddenly, she fell off a cliff. Her body exploded. She cried out as waves of ecstasy crashed around her, and she flew.

Quickly sheathing himself in a condom from the bedstand, he positioned himself between her legs. With a single rough thrust, he shoved himself all the way inside her. Gripping his shoulders, Bree cried out as sudden pain tore through her pleasure.

When Vladimir felt the barrier he hadn't expected, he froze, looking down at her in shock.

"You were—a virgin?" he breathed.

Bree's eyes squeezed shut, her beautiful face full of anguish as she turned it away, as if she didn't want him to see. He didn't move, unable to fathom the evidence he'd felt with his own body. "Why didn't you tell me?"

Trembling beneath him, she slowly opened her eyes again—limpid hazel eyes that glimmered like an autumn lake dark with rain. "I did," she whispered. She took a ragged breath. "You didn't believe me."

Vladimir stared at her beautiful face. Around him, the whole world suddenly seemed to shake and rattle. But the earthquake was in his own heart. He felt something crack inside his soul.

Everything he'd thought about Bree was wrong.

Everything he'd believed her to be—*wrong.*

With a ragged intake of breath, he pulled away. Sitting back on the bed, he choked out, "I don't understand."

"Don't you?" She sat up against the headboard, and her eyes shimmered in the silver-gold moonlight dappling the high-ceilinged bedroom. She licked her lips. "When you didn't believe me, I started hoping I could keep my virginity a secret. So you wouldn't…"

She stopped.

"So I wouldn't what?"

Her lips trembled as she tried to smile. "Well, it's pathetic, isn't it?" She didn't try to cover her nakedness, as another woman might have done. She just looked straight into his eyes, without artifice, without defenses. "There was no other man for me. Not before you. And not after."

Staring at her, Vladimir felt as if he'd just been sucker punched.

She'd told him the truth. All these years he'd thought of Bree Dalton as a liar, or worse. But even when she'd looked him in the eyes and told him she was a virgin, he hadn't believed her.

Who was the one who didn't recognize the truth when he saw it?

Who was the one who'd forgotten how?

Setting his jaw, he looked at her grimly. "And Alaska?"

She looked down, her eyelashes a dark sweep against her pale skin. "Everything your brother tried to tell you, that Christmas night he burst in on us, was true," she said softly. "I never had the rights to sell Josie's land. I was trying to distract you, so you'd put down earnest money in cash before you realized it, and my sister and I could disappear into a new life."

"To con people somewhere else."

"It was all I knew how to do." Bree lifted her gaze. "It never occurred to me that I could change. Not until…"

Her voice trailed off.

Yes, Vladimir, I'll marry you. He could almost hear her joyful, choked voice that Christmas night, see the tears in her beautiful eyes as she'd thrown her arms around him and whispered, "I'm not good enough for you, not by half. But I'll spend the rest of my life trying to be."

Now, his hands tightened into fists. "You had plenty of chances to tell me the truth. Instead, you let me find out about your con from Kasimir. You let me shout at him and throw him out of your cabin as a damned liar. You let me leave that night, still not knowing the truth. Until I started getting phone calls the next morning, and discovered from reporters that everything he'd told me about you was true."

"I wanted to tell you. But I was afraid."

"Afraid," he sneered.

"Yes," she cried. "Afraid you wouldn't listen to my side. That you'd abandon me, and I'd be left with no money and no defenses against the wolves circling us. I was afraid," she whispered, "you'd stop loving me."

That was exactly what had happened.

"If that is true, and you were truly intending to change purely because of this *love* for me," he said, his voice dripping scorn, "why didn't you go back to your old life of cheating and lying the instant I left?"

Her eyes widened, then fell. "It wasn't just for you," she muttered. "It was for me, too." She looked up. "And Josie. I wanted to be a good example. I wanted us to live a safe, boring, respectable life." Hugging her knees to her chest, she blinked fast, her eyes suspiciously wet. "But we couldn't."

"You couldn't be respectable?"

"We never felt safe." She licked her lips. "Back in Alaska, some men had threatened to hurt us if I didn't replace money we'd stolen. But my father had already spent it all and more. It was a million dollars, impossible to repay. So for the last ten years, I made sure we stayed off the radar. No job promotions. No college for Josie. Never staying too long anywhere." Bree's lips twisted. "Not much of a life, but at least no legs got broken."

His hands clenched as he remembered the angry looks of the players at the poker game, when she'd told them how she'd cheated them. "Why didn't you tell me about this?"

"I did," she said, bewildered at his reaction. "A few times."

"You told me you had debts," he said tightly. "Everyone

has debts. You didn't tell me some men were threatening to break your legs."

She took a deep breath, her face filled with pain.

"Not mine," she whispered. "Josie's."

Vladimir rose to his feet. Still naked, he paced three steps, clenching his hands. His shoulders felt so tense they burned. He was having a physical reaction.

If he'd been wrong about Bree, what else had he been wrong about?

He stopped as he remembered his brother's face, contorted beneath the lights of the Christmas tree. *You're taking her word over mine? You just met this girl two months ago. I've looked up to you my whole life. Why can't you believe I might know more than you—just once?*

But Vladimir, two years older, had always been the leader, the protector. He could still remember six-year-old Kasimir panting as he struggled through the snowy two miles to school. *Wait for me, Volodya! Wait for me!*

But he'd never waited. *If you want to follow me, keep up, Kasimir. Stop being slow.*

Now, as Vladimir remembered that long-lost adoration in his brother's eyes, his heart gave a strange, sickening jump in his chest. Tightening his jaw, he pushed the memory away. He looked at Bree.

"No one will ever threaten you or yours again."

Her lips parted. "What will you do?"

He narrowed his eyes. "They threatened to break a child's legs," he said roughly. "So I'll break every bone in their bodies. First their legs. Then their arms. Then—"

"Who are you?" she cried.

He stopped, surprised at the horror on her face. "What?"

"You're so ruthless." She swallowed. "There is no mercy in you. It's true what they say."

"You expect me to, what—give them a cookie and tuck them into bed?"

"No, but—" she spread her arms helplessly "—break every single bone? You don't just want to win, you want to crush them. Torture them. You've become the kind of man who…" Her eyes seared his. "Who'd destroy his own brother."

For a moment, Vladimir was speechless. Then he glared at her. "Kasimir made his own choice. When I wouldn't listen to his words about you, he told the story to a reporter. He betrayed me, and when I suggested we split up our partnership, it was his choice to agree—"

"You deliberately cheated your own brother," she interrupted, "out of millions of dollars. And you've spent ten years trying to destroy him. You don't just get revenge, Vladimir. You deal a double dose of pain—breaking not just their legs, but their arms!"

Pacing two steps, he clawed back his dark hair angrily. "What would you have me do, Breanna? Let them threaten you? Pay them off? Let them win? Let my brother take over my company? Not defend myself?"

"But you don't just defend yourself," she said. "You're ruthless. And you revel in it." Her eyes lifted to his. "Has it made you happy, Vladimir? Has destroying other people's lives made yours better?"

He flashed hot, then cold. As they faced each other, naked without touching, in a bedroom deep with shadows and frosted with moonlight, a mixture of emotions raced through his bloodstream that he hadn't felt in a long, long time—emotions he could barely recognize.

Bree took a deep, ragged breath.

"I loved you. I loved the honest, openhearted man you were." Tears glistened like icicles against her pale skin. "The truth is, I love him still."

Vladimir sucked in his breath. *What was she saying?*

"But the man you are now…" She looked at him. "I hate the man you've become, Vladimir," she whispered. "I hate you now. With all my heart."

He took a single staggering step. He held out his hand and heard his own hoarse, shaking voice. "Bree…"

"No!" She nearly fell off the bed to avoid his touch. Snatching the crumpled, pink silk robe off the floor, she covered her naked body. "I should never have let you touch me. Ever!"

She fled from the bedroom, racing down the hall.

For an instant, Vladimir stood frozen, paralyzed with shock.

Then, narrowing his eyes, he yanked on a pair of jeans and followed her grimly. Downstairs, he heard the door that led to the pool bang. He followed the sound outside. From the corner of his eye, beneath dark silhouettes of palm trees against the sapphire sky, he saw a pale flash going down the cliff toward the beach.

He followed. Striding around the pool, he pushed through the gate and went down steps chiseled into the rock, leading to the private, white-sand beach. At the bottom, surrounded by the noisy roar of the surf lapping the sand at his feet, he looked right and left.

Where was she?

The large Hawaiian moon glowed like an opalescent pearl across the dark blue velvet ocean, its light sparkling like diamonds.

I loved the honest, openhearted man you were. Her poignant words echoed in his mind. *I hate the man you've become.*

Closing his eyes, he thought of how he'd spent the past ten years, constantly proving to himself how hard and heartless he could be. Betraying others before they could even *think* of turning on him.

Half the world called him ruthless; the other half called him corrupt. Vladimir had worn their hatred like a badge of honor. He'd told himself that it was the fate of every powerful man to be despised. It only proved he'd succeeded. He'd conquered the world. He'd just never thought it would be so…

Meaningless. Bleakly, he looked out toward the dark waves of the Pacific.

Has it made you happy? Has destroying other people's lives made yours better?

The warm breeze felt cool against his bare skin. He'd loved her so recklessly. The night he'd proposed to her, in front of the crackling fire that dark, cold Christmas, had been the happiest of his life.

Until Kasimir had burst into her cabin and called Vladimir a fool for falling into a con woman's trap. The fighting had woken up her kid sister upstairs, so after tossing his brother out, he'd gone back to his hotel alone. He'd been woken by the ringing of his cell phone—and questions from a *Wall Street Journal* reporter.

Vladimir put a hand to his forehead.

For the past ten years, this woman he'd called a liar and a whore had been quietly working minimum-wage jobs, in a desperate attempt to provide an honest life for her young sister. While he…

Vladimir exhaled. He'd done exactly what she said. He'd cut all mercy from his heart, to make damn sure no one ever made a fool of him again. He'd closed himself off completely from every human feeling, and he'd tried to eradicate the memory of the woman who'd once broken him.

The moon retreated behind a cloud, and he saw a shadow move. He stumbled down the beach, and as the moon burst out of the darkness, he saw her.

Silvery light frosted the dark silhouette of her body as she rose like Venus from the waves. His heart twisted in his chest.

Breanna.

CHAPTER SIX

BREE stood alone in the surf, staring bleakly out at the moonlit ocean, wishing she was far, far away from Hawaii. She felt the waves against her bare thighs, felt the sand squish beneath her toes. She shivered in the warm night, wishing she was a million miles away.

How could she have given him her virginity?

How could she have let him kiss her, touch her, make her explode with pleasure? *How?*

Allowing Vladimir to make love to her had brought back all the memories of the way she'd once loved him. How could she have allowed herself to be so vulnerable? Why hadn't she been able to protect herself, to keep her heart cold?

Because he'd always known how to get past all her defenses. Always. He hadn't forced her. He hadn't needed to. All he'd done was kiss her, and she'd surrendered, melting into his arms. And she'd been able to hold nothing back. Her feelings had come pouring out of her lips. How she'd loved him.

How she hated him.

When Vladimir had said that no one would ever threaten her or Josie again, she'd been relieved. Grateful, even. Then he'd spoken with such relish about breaking all their bones.

Bree had no love for the men who'd made their lives a misery over the past ten years. But she would have paid back every penny if she could. And seeing Vladimir, the prince she'd loved at eighteen, turned into this…this *monster*…was unbearable.

She'd thought the man she'd loved had betrayed her. But it was far worse than that.

The charming, tender-hearted man she'd loved was dead. Dead and gone forever. And left in his place was nothing but a selfish, coldhearted tycoon.

She missed the man she'd loved. She missed him as she hadn't allowed herself to do for a full ten years. The way he'd held her, respected her, the way he'd made her laugh. He'd still been strong, but he'd looked out for those weaker than himself.

But that man was gone—gone forever.

Tears streamed unchecked down her cheeks as she bowed her head and cried in the moonlight. Even the cool water of the ocean couldn't wash away her grief and regret.

For all these years, she'd pompously lectured Josie that she must be strong as a woman—must never give a man power over her. Bree wiped her eyes.

She was a fraud. She wasn't strong. She never had been.

"Breanna."

She heard his low, deep voice behind her. Whirling around with a gasp, she saw him walking at the edge of the surf, coming toward her.

"Vladimir," she whispered, taking an involuntary step back into the ocean. "You followed me?"

"I couldn't let you go." He walked straight into the waves, never looking away from her. Moonlight traced the strong muscles of his naked chest, and the dark hairline leading to the low-slung waistband of his jeans.

She folded her trembling arms over her wet, flimsy robe. "What more could you possibly do to hurt me?"

His eyes were dark and hot, his voice low. "I don't want to hurt you. Not anymore. Never again."

"Then what do you want?" Then suddenly, Bree knew, and her body shook all over. Backing away, she held up her hand. "Don't—don't come any closer!"

But he didn't stop. He waded nearer, until the water rose

higher than his thighs, to his lean, sexy hips, where the wet jeans clung.

Vladimir's gaze fell to her body. Looking down, she realized her robe was completely soaked and sticking to her skin. Even in the moonlight, the color of her nipples was visible through the translucent, diaphanous pink silk.

They stood inches apart, waist-deep in the ocean. Their eyes locked. A current of electricity flashed through her.

"I won't be your possession, Vladimir," she whispered. "I won't be your slave."

His lips curved. "How could a woman like you," he said, "ever be any man's slave?"

A large wave pushed her forward, and the palm she'd held out against him fell upon the hot, bare skin of his solid chest. Without moving her hand, Bree looked up at him. Her heart was beating wildly.

"But you're mine." His dark eyes gleamed as, grabbing her wrists, he pulled her tightly against his body. Twining his hands through her wet hair, he cupped her face and tilted her mouth upwards. "You've always been mine."

"I'm not—"

"Your own body proved it. You belong to me, Breanna. Admit it."

She shook her head wildly. "I despise you."

"Perhaps I deserve your hatred." His words were low, barely audible over the surf and the plaintive cry of faraway seagulls. "But you belong to me, just the same. And I'm going to take you."

As the surf thundered against the beach, Vladimir lowered his mouth to hers.

His kiss was searing, passionate. But she realized something had changed. As he held her against his body like a newly discovered treasure, his lips were exploratory, even tender. His kiss was full of yearning and heartbreak—of vulnerability.

It was the kiss she remembered. The exact way Vladimir had kissed her when Bree's world had been reborn.

A choked sob came from the back of her throat. Wrapping her arms around his shoulders, she kissed him back with all the aching passion of lost time. Standing on the edge of the moon-drenched ocean, they clung to each other as the waves tried, but failed, to pull them apart.

Without a word, he lifted her against his naked chest. Their wet bodies dripped water as he carried her out of the ocean, back to the white-sand beach. And as he carried her up the moonlit cliff path that led to the villa, she closed her eyes, clinging to him.

You're mine. You've always been mine. Your own body proved it.

It was true. Even though she hated him, it had always been true.

Bree was his. And whether she wished it or not, she always would be.

Vladimir left a trail of sand and water as he crossed the floor of their bedroom, then gently lowered Bree to her feet beside the bed.

Neither of them spoke. Almost holding his breath, he slowly stroked down her soft arms to her slender waist. He undid the silken tie of her robe. Never taking his eyes from hers, he peeled the wet, translucent silk off her shoulders and dropped it to the floor.

She now stood before him naked and beautiful, her eyes luminous in the moonlight. Looking at her, this sensual angel, Vladimir trembled, racked with desires both sacred and profane.

He'd taken her virginity. He couldn't undo that.

But he could change her memory of it.

Pulling her naked body into his arms, against his bare chest, he cupped the back of her head, tangling his hands in her long wet hair, and lowered his mouth to hers.

This time, without so much anger and prejudice in his heart, he finally felt her inexperience, the way she held her breath as she hesitated, her lips shy, then tried to follow his lead. He noticed everything he hadn't wanted to see.

This time, he did not plunder. He kissed her softly. Slowly. His lips suggested, rather than forced; they taught, rather than demanded. He let her set the pace. He felt her small body tremble in his arms, and then, with a deep sigh from the back of her throat, she relaxed. Her arms reached around his neck, and he felt her mouth part for him, offering freely what he'd earlier taken like a brute.

As Vladimir held her naked, soft form, still wet from the ocean, waves of desire pummeled his own body with need. But he controlled himself. He would not take her roughly. This time, he would give her the perfect pleasure she deserved. The night he'd wanted to give her long ago...

Standing beside the four-poster bed, he kissed her for a long time, holding her tight. The two of them swayed in the shadows of the bedroom. Her soft breasts felt like silk, brushing against his bare chest. His ran his hands over the smooth, warm skin of her back, beneath her wet hair.

Their kiss deepened. He did not force it, and neither did she. It just happened, like magic, as the hunger grew like fire between them. He felt the tip of her tongue brush his, and his whole body suddenly felt electric. He could almost see colors in bursts of light behind his closed eyes, like an illumination in the darkness. She was his guiding light and North Star. His one true point.

He held on to her as if, by kissing her, he could go back in time and be the openhearted young man he'd once been. The fearless one...

Bree's hands moved slowly down the sides of his body, paus-

❧HARLEQUIN® READER SERVICE—Here's How It Works:

Accepting your 2 free books and 2 free gifts (gifts valued at approximately $10.00) places you under no obligation to buy anything. You may keep the books and gifts and return the shipping statement marked "cancel." If you do not cancel, about a month later we'll send you 6 additional books and bill you just $4.30 each for the regular-print edition or $4.80 each for the larger-print edition in the U.S. or $4.99 each for the regular-print edition or $5.49 each for the larger-print edition in Canada. That's a savings of at least 13% off the cover price. It's quite a bargain! Shipping and handling is just 50¢ per book in the U.S. and 75¢ per book in Canada.* You may cancel at any time, but if you choose to continue, every month we'll send you 6 more books, which you may either purchase at the discount price or return to us and cancel your subscription.

*Terms and prices subject to change without notice. Prices do not include applicable taxes. Sales tax applicable in N.Y. Canadian residents will be charged applicable taxes. Offer not valid in Quebec. All orders subject to credit approval. Credit or debit balances in a customer's account(s) may be offset by any other outstanding balance owed by or to the customer. Please allow 4 to 6 weeks for delivery. Offer available while quantities last.

NO POSTAGE
NECESSARY
IF MAILED
IN THE
UNITED STATES

BUSINESS REPLY MAIL
FIRST-CLASS MAIL   PERMIT NO. 717   BUFFALO, NY

POSTAGE WILL BE PAID BY ADDRESSEE

HARLEQUIN READER SERVICE
PO BOX 1867
BUFFALO NY 14240-9952

If offer card is missing write to: Harlequin Reader Service, P.O. Box 1867, Buffalo NY 14240-1867 or visit www.ReaderService.com

HP-L7-02/13

GET FREE BOOKS and FREE GIFTS
WHEN YOU PLAY THE...

Lucky 7

Just scratch off the silver box with a coin. Then check below to see the gifts you get!

SLOT MACHINE GAME!

YES!

I have scratched off the silver box. Please send me the 2 free Harlequin Presents® books and 2 free gifts for which I qualify. I understand I am under no obligation to purchase any books, as explained on the back of this card.

❑ I prefer the regular-print edition
106/306 HDL FV9T

❑ I prefer the larger-print edition
176/376 HDL FV9T

FIRST NAME   LAST NAME

ADDRESS

APT.#   CITY

STATE/PROV.   ZIP/POSTAL CODE

7 7 7	**Worth TWO FREE BOOKS plus 2 FREE Mystery Gifts!**
🍒 🍒 🍒	**Worth TWO FREE BOOKS!**
♣ ♣ ♣	**Worth ONE FREE BOOK!**
🔔 🔔 🍒	**TRY AGAIN!**

Visit us at:
www.ReaderService.com

HP-L7-02/13

Offer limited to one per household and not applicable to series that subscriber is currently receiving.

Your Privacy—The Harlequin® Reader Service is committed to protecting your privacy. Our Privacy Policy is available online at www.ReaderService.com or upon request from the Harlequin Reader Service. We make a portion of our mailing list available to reputable third parties that offer products we believe may interest you. If you prefer that we not exchange your name with third parties, or if you wish to clarify or modify your communication preferences, please visit us at www.ReaderService.com/consumerchoice or write to us at Harlequin Reader Service Preference Service, P.O. Box 9062, Buffalo, NY 14269. Include your complete name and address.

DETACH AND MAIL CARD TODAY!

Printed in the U.S.A. ®and ™ are trademarks owned and used by the trademark owner and/or its licensee.

© 2012 HARLEQUIN ENTERPRISES LIMITED

HP-L7-02/13

ing at the recent scars. She drew back to look at his skin. "The racing accident did this?"

He didn't trust himself to speak, so he gave a single unsteady nod.

Her fingers traced the other scars she saw. "And this?"

"Boxing."

"And this?"

"Skydiving."

"So reckless," she sighed. "Don't you know you could die?"

"We're all going to die," he said roughly. "I was trying to feel alive."

Her fingertips explored, accepted fully. As she touched his scars, he held his breath, feeling his soul laid bare.

"Still sorry the car accident didn't kill me?" he said in a low voice.

She stopped at the waistband of his jeans and looked up at him with troubled eyes. For a moment, she didn't answer. Then she shook her head, moving her hand over his heart.

"No," she whispered. "Because I think the man I loved is still inside you."

He grabbed her wrist. "He's dead and gone."

She raised her eyes.

"Are you sure?" she said softly.

The look in her hazel eyes made Vladimir's heart twist in his chest. It was as if she knew exactly who he was, scars and all. As if she saw right through him. Straight to his broken soul.

Turning away without a word, he unzipped the fly of his jeans. He wrestled the wet denim to the floor. Grabbing her wrists, he pulled her to the bed, with her naked body on top of his. The feeling of having her like this—Breanna, the woman he'd hated for ten years, the first and last woman he'd let himself love—left him dizzy.

"I'm not that man," he said aloud, to both of them.

Pulling her wrists from his grip, she put her hands on either side of his face.

"Let me see," she whispered. Lowering her head, she kissed him.

As her sweet mouth moved against his lips, the weight of her naked body pressed against him, and it felt like heaven. Her hands moved slowly across his skin, down his arms, to his hips. Lowering her head, she followed the same path, kissing down his chest to his flat belly.

When he felt the heat of her breath against his thighs, he squeezed his eyes shut, suddenly afraid to move. She paused. Then, tentatively, she reached out her hand and stroked him, exploring the length of his shaft. He gasped softly. Then he felt her weight move on the bed, and suddenly her lips and breath were on him. He felt her mouth against him, her tongue stroke his shaft to the tip.

He gasped again.

She moved slowly, and he suddenly realized this was new to her; she'd never explored any man so intimately before. The thought of this—that she'd waited all this time for him, only for him—was too much for him to endure. He felt her soft warm mouth enfold him, and he sucked in his breath. One more flicker of her tongue—

Sitting up, he grabbed her, rolling her over. Lying on top of her, he looked straight into her eyes and breathed hoarsely, "No, Breanna. No."

Putting his hand on her cheek, he lowered his head to hers. As he kissed her lips, his hands stroked her satin-soft skin, cupping her breasts. Moving down her body, he kissed first one breast, then the other, with hot need, suckling her until she gasped. His fingertips caressed down her belly. When he reached the mound between her legs, he stopped. His body was shaking, screaming for him to push inside her.

But he did not. He moved abruptly to the bottom of the bed. Taking one of her feet in his hands, he slowly kissed it, suckling her toes, tasting salt from the Pacific on her sweet, warm skin. He felt her tremble as he kissed the hollow of her foot, then moved up her leg to her calf, and the tender spot behind her knee. When he reached her thighs, he pressed them apart, spreading her.

He risked a glance upward. Her face was rapt, her eyes tightly closed. He heard the rasp of her breath and felt the tremble of her legs as she nervously tried to close them. Smiling to himself—he could hardly wait to give her this pleasure—he held her legs splayed and kissed slowly up the soft skin of her thighs. He moved higher and higher, teasing her with his breath, until he finally spread her wide. Lowering his head, he took a long, deep taste.

He had the satisfaction of hearing her cry out as her body shook with need. Slowly, deliberately, he moved his tongue, widening it to lap at her, then pointing the tip to penetrate a half inch inside her. He felt her body get tighter and tighter, saw her back start to arch off the mattress, as before. But this time, he wanted to give her more.

Flicking his tongue against her swollen nub, he pushed a thick knuckle of his folded finger just barely inside her. She felt wet, so wet for him. One of her hands rested on his head, clutching his hair, no longer trying to pull him away, embarrassment and fear forgotten beneath the waves of pleasure. Her other hand gripped the tousled white sheets of the bed. Her body grew tense and tenser beneath him, until she started to lift off the mattress, as if gravity itself were losing power over her. She held her breath, and then with a loud cry, she exploded. He felt her body contract hard around his knuckle.

Sheathing himself in another condom—except this time, his hands shook so badly he nearly dropped it—he positioned himself as she was still gasping in kittenish cries of pleasure. He wanted to plunge himself inside her.

But *he did not*.

Even now, he forced himself to stay in control. He entered her body inch by inch, stretching her wide to fully accept him, doing it slowly, so that she could feel him inside her, and he could feel every inch of her. Her eyes opened with wonder, locking with his own. They never looked away as he slowly filled her, so slowly that the exquisite pleasure almost felt like pain. He finally pushed himself inside her, all the way to the hilt.

And he forgot to breathe. She felt so good. This was ecstasy he'd never felt before. *Faster,* his body screamed. *Harder, faster, deeper, now!*

But with a will of iron, he gritted his teeth and ignored his body's demand. He forced himself to go slow for her, in a way he'd never done before for any woman. He wanted this to be what she would remember from her first night of making love. Not the ruthless, rough, crude way of before.

Gripping her hips to steady his pace, he started to slowly ride her. Her hands held his backside, pulling him more tightly inside her, deeper, and deeper still.

He felt her body tighten again, and as he lowered his head to suckle her breasts—first one, then the other—his hardened body moved in a circular motion against hers as he thrust inside her.

Closing her eyes, she clutched his shoulders, digging her nails into his flesh. Vladimir's heart was pounding in his throat with the need to explode inside her, but he forced himself to relax, to wait. He just needed to see her face light up, to hear her gasp. He just needed to feel her tighten around him one more time….

He pounded inside her, harder and deeper, and her hips lifted to meet the force of his thrust. Lowering his head once more, he kissed her. As their lips met, he heard her suck in her breath, felt her body tighten….

And then she screamed, even louder than she had before. In that same instant, he finally let himself go. It felt so good…. So good…

Stars exploded behind his eyes, and his own ecstatic shout

rang in his ears. Their joined cries of pleasure echoed in the quiet moonlit night, louder than the distant roar of the sea.

Afterwards, they collapsed into each other's arms. Exhausted, he held her close, kissing her temple, whispering her name like a prayer. "Breanna…"

Vladimir woke abruptly when he heard his cell phone ringing. Blinking in surprise, he saw gray dawn breaking over the clouds. He'd slept all night in Bree's arms.

He looked down. She was still sleeping, cradled naked against his chest.

He'd lowered his guard and slept with a woman in his arms—something he'd never been able to do with anyone but her. The tension in his shoulders was gone. His head didn't hurt. His heartbeat was soft and slow. It was the best sleep he'd had since the accident.

Was this what peace felt like?

His phone buzzed again. Getting up quietly from bed, he picked it up from the nightstand and left the bedroom. Closing the door silently behind him, not wanting to wake her, he put the phone to his ear. "Yes?"

"Your Highness." It was John Anderson, his chief of operations. "The Arctic Oil merger is now urgent. Your brother just had a huge oil find in Alaska. On the land he bought last spring from that Spaniard, Eduardo Cruz."

"Wait," Vladimir growled. His hands were shaking as he went down the hall to his office. So much for peace. He could feel his heartbeat thrumming in his neck, hear his own blood rushing in his ears. His brother had that effect on him. He closed the office door. "Go."

"Sir, if the find is as substantial as it seems, oil might soon flood the market, causing the price to drop…."

Vladimir paced as he listened, clawing back his hair. Usually business calmed him, because he relished a fight. But not when the news involved his brother.

Volodya, Volodya, please wait for me! Closing his eyes,

Vladimir could still see his baby brother's chubby face as he'd toddled after him through the snow those long-ago, hungry winters. Sometimes supplies at the homestead grew lean, and Vladimir had gone out with their father to hunt rabbits. *I want to hunt, too.* Once, Kasimir had idolized his big brother. Now, he enjoyed taunting and hurting Vladimir any chance he could get. Kasimir would probably be the death of him.

As his COO droned on, Vladimir barely listened. He felt weary. For ten years now, he'd fought this fight. There was no longer any joy in it. He'd taken up hobbies like car racing, risking death for the sake of cutting a few seconds off his time. He'd taken women, in endless, meaningless one-night stands. He'd been starving to feel something. Anything. But lately, even the thrill of cheating death had brought only a tiny blip.

There were no new worlds to conquer. He'd been going through the motions for a long time. He felt nothing.

Not until last night.

Not until Breanna returned to him.

He exhaled. *Breanna.*

She made him *feel,* after years of deadness. She'd brought pleasure. Yearning. Anger. Guilt. Desire. All wrapped up in a chaotic ball. He felt as if he'd just woken out of a coma, after years of dull gray sleep.

Perhaps he was incapable of love, with a soul twisted and gnarled like a tree split by lightning. He'd told her the truth: he'd never be the man he'd once been—naive and trusting enough to give away the shirt off his back. Not even for a woman like her.

Barely hearing his COO's voice, Vladimir looked through the window of his villa's home office. The bright Hawaiian dawn was burning through the low-swept morning clouds still kissing the green earth. The sky was turning blue, as blue as the sparkling ocean below.

He had the sudden memory of Breanna rising from the waves in the moonlight last night, her short silk robe stuck to her like a second skin as rivulets of water streamed down her breasts to her thighs. Vladimir shuddered, turning instantly hard. Instead of satiating him, making love to her had only increased his hunger.

"…So what should we do, Your Highness?" his COO finished anxiously.

Vladimir blinked, realizing he hadn't been listening to the man for the past ten minutes. But he suddenly felt bored by business matters—completely bored. Even though it involved his brother. "What is your opinion?"

"We'll have someone at our Alaska site infiltrate your brother's mining operation to see if the data is accurate. If it is, we can try to influence the political process to delay their building. We could even consider some kind of sabotage at the mine. Although of course it would in no way be traceable back to you, sir…."

You're ruthless. And you revel in it. The realization of how low he'd sunk caused Vladimir to flinch. "No."

"But, Your Highness…"

"I said no." Clawing back his hair, he paced across his office with his phone at his ear, prowling in circles around his desk.

"So what are your orders, Your Highness? How shall we make sure your brother does not succeed?"

Vladimir abruptly stopped. He'd been wrong about Breanna.

Could he have similarly been wrong about Kasimir, overreacting to his brother's betrayal?

It was an accident. His brother's voice had been muffled, humble, on the phone the next day from St. Petersburg. *When you wouldn't believe me, I was angry and drunk at the airport bar. I didn't realize the man sitting next to me was a reporter for the* Anchorage Herald. *Forgive me, Volodya.*

Vladimir's hands tightened into fists. But he hadn't accepted the apology. He'd been angry, humiliated, haunted. And he feared his stupidity might jeopardize the Siberian mining rights that were about to come through, rights that could make or break the fledgling company. "If you can't trust my leadership, we should end this partnership."

"Leadership? I thought we were supposed to be equals," his brother had retorted. When Vladimir maintained a frosty silence, Kasimir had said harshly, "Fine. I'll keep the rights in Africa and South America. And you can go to hell."

Vladimir had been angry enough to let his brother go without telling him about the Siberian rights worth potentially half a billion dollars. He'd effectively cheated Kasimir out of his half.

Perhaps... He took a deep breath. Perhaps Kasimir had some cause to seek revenge against him.

"You will do nothing." Now, Vladimir stared out the window toward the palm trees and blue sky. "My brother's operation in Alaska does not affect us. Leave him alone. May the best company win."

"But, sir!"

"Xendzov Mining can win in a fair fight."

"Of course we can!" the man replied indignantly. He continued in a bewildered voice, "It's just that we've never tried."

"No more dirty tricks," Vladimir said harshly.

"It will be harder—"

"Deal with it."

The man cleared his throat. "You were expected in St. Petersburg today for the signing of the Arctic Oil merger. How long do you wish us to delay...?"

Vladimir gritted his teeth. "I will be at the office tomorrow."

"Good." He audibly exhaled. "With ten billion dollars on the line, we don't want anything to—"

"Tomorrow." Vladimir hung up. Tossing his phone on his desk, he left the study, with its computers and piles of paperwork. Walking outside to the courtyard, he stopped by the pool. Closing his eyes, he turned his face toward the bright morning sun. He felt the warmth of the golden light, and took a breath of the exotic, flower-scented air.

I think the man I love is still inside you.

He's dead and gone.

Are you sure?

Slowly, Vladimir opened his eyes. He looked up at the twenty-million-dollar mansion that he'd bought as a refuge, but which had felt like a prison.

Bree Dalton had brought it to life. As she'd done to him.

But what right did he have to keep her prisoner?

He'd told himself she deserved it. She was the one who'd betrayed him ten years ago, then foolishly wagered her body in a card game. Let her finally face the consequences of her actions.

He paced around the edge of the pool, then stopped, clawing back his hair. But she'd offered her body in desperation. He'd abandoned her without a penny in Alaska, with men threatening them for money. And yet, even under that pressure, Bree had managed to come through the fire with a soul as pure as steel.

He still wanted to find those men and break their legs, their arms. Every bone in their bodies. But there was something he wanted even more.

He wanted Breanna.

His long-dormant conscience stirred, telling him he had no right to keep her. If he truly believed that she'd never meant to betray him, that she'd wagered herself only to protect her little sister, then he should let her go. If he kept her as his slave, it would make him no better than the criminals who'd imprisoned her with debts. He was selfish, but not a monster.

Wasn't he?

Pushing the thought away, he pulled out his cell phone and made a few calls. One to an investigator. The other to his secretary, to arrange a Russian visa. Then he picked a wild orchid from the garden and went back inside the house. He'd given his household staff the day off, after Mrs. Kalani's reaction to his treatment of Bree yesterday. So the enormous kitchen was quiet as he made her a breakfast tray. Putting the orchid in a vase, he walked up the stairs to their bedroom.

Breanna was still drowsing in bed. But as he pushed open the door, she sat up, tucking the sheet modestly over her naked breasts.

"Good morning," she said shyly.

Vladimir went to the bed. She looked so innocent and fresh and pretty, the epitome of everything good. He put the breakfast tray into her lap. "I thought you might be hungry."

"I am." Her cheeks blushed a soft pink as she looked down at the tray, with its toast and fresh fruit and fragrant flower. "Thank you." Looking up, she gave him a sudden wicked smile. "Last night left me really, really hungry."

The bright, teasing look on her face took his breath away. He said abruptly, "I have to go to St. Petersburg today."

Her face fell. "Oh." Looking away, she said stiffly, "Well. Good. I'll be glad to be free of you."

"Too bad." Turning her face roughly, he cupped her cheek. "You're coming with me."

Her eyes lit up. Then she scowled, glaring at him. "Because I'm your property and slave, right? Because you get to boss me around and take me wherever you want, right?"

He kissed her bare shoulder. "You got it."

She shivered as his lips touched her. "You are such a jerk—"

Leaning over the tray, he kissed her lips, long and thoroughly, just to remind her who was in charge. Her lips parted so sweetly, it took all his strength to stop. He needed to order his private jet to leave within the hour. He had no time to make love to her.

But as he drew away, he saw that the white cotton sheet had fallen from her heedless hands, revealing the glory of her naked, trembling breasts. Against his will, he leaned forward to kiss her again, and they both jumped as they heard the breakfast tray crash to the floor.

Bree gave an impish laugh. "Maybe you should consider paper plates. I know you're rich and all, but honestly, I can't clean up all your broken china."

With a growl, Vladimir pushed her back against the bed.

"Don't worry. You'll never clean for me again," he whispered. "From now on…there's only one thing I want you to do for me."

Forcing his conscience to be silent, he lowered his mouth to hers. As he tasted the sweetness of her lips, he knew he wouldn't give her up. She was his. He'd won her—she belonged to him, for as long as he desired her. If that meant he was a monster, so be it.

I think the man I love is still inside you.

He's dead and gone.

Are you sure?

As Vladimir felt her naked body move like silk beneath him, she gave a trembling sigh. She wrapped her arms around his neck and pulled him down to heaven.

Yes. He was sure.

CHAPTER SEVEN

Russia.

As a child, Bree had traveled down the rocky, forest-covered Alaskan coast with her father, seeking gullible tourists off cruise ships for poker games. Her favorite village had been Sitka, once the capital of Russian America. At twelve, she'd looked across the gray, frozen Bering Sea and dreamed of the distant, ancient, mysterious land of the tsars.

When wooden Orthodox churches were being hacked out of the wilderness in Alaska, St. Petersburg was already a century old, built on the orders of a tsar. She'd dreamed of someday seeing the palatial Russian city, the onion domes of its cathedrals shining with silver and gold.

But Bree never dreamed she'd come here as the cosseted mistress of a prince. For two days now, she'd been living in his three-story palace outside the city, built like a fortress on a hill, overlooking the Gulf of Finland on the Baltic Sea. She'd spent her days shopping in the most exclusive boutiques of the city, accompanied by his bodyguards and his chauffeur.

She spent her nights in Vladimir's bed. He came to her in the middle of the night, waking her, making love to her in darkness, setting her body ablaze from the inside out. He burned her with the fire of their mutual need. Each night, she fell asleep in his arms, satiated with pleasure.

But each day, she woke up in the cold gray winter dawn, bereft and alone.

Vladimir was extremely busy, working on the Arctic Oil merger. Even if he was using her only for sex, she shouldn't take it personally. Right? That was what she'd expected. Wasn't it? She should be grateful for this life he'd given her, one of luxury, pleasure and comfort. Most women would envy her. She should make the best of things.

So she tried.

Left alone all day, she went shopping, as Vladimir had ordered. Four bodyguards took her out in a black limousine with bulletproof glass. Expensive designer shops closed their doors to all other customers so Bree could shop alone, quite alone, with only sycophantic store clerks for company.

Maybe it would have been fun if Vladimir had been with her. Or Josie. Bree missed her sister like a physical ache in her heart. She'd tried multiple times over the past few days to call her, but Josie never answered. Bree tried to squelch her worries. Surely Josie was fine. It was just her own loneliness, playing tricks on her mood, that made Bree anxious.

But after two exhausting days of shopping, shocked at the outrageous prices, she was desperate to find something, anything, else to do. "Buy a wardrobe of winter clothes," Vladimir had said, shoving his credit card into her hand. "And lingerie." Wanting to be done, she'd randomly grabbed two items the clerks were pushing on her—a long, puffy black coat and an expensive lingerie set with a white lace bustier, G-string and garter belt—and practically ran from the store. The bodyguards formed a tunnel to her waiting black limo, and she fled past the annoyed faces of Russian women waiting outside.

But now, on her third day in St. Petersburg, as she sat alone at a very long table in the empty palace, eating an elegant lunch prepared by the Russian-speaking housekeeper, Bree felt a rush of pure relief when her cell phone rang. She snatched it up. "Hello?"

"What are you wearing?"

At the sound of Vladimir's low, sensual voice, her shoulders relaxed. "I thought you might be Josie."

"Sorry to disappoint you."

"I'm glad to hear your voice." Her hand tightened on her phone. "I'm, um, wearing my old flannel pajamas and big bootie slippers from home."

"Sounds sexy. Want to come over?"

"Come where?"

"To my office."

She blinked. "Why?"

"I have a fifteen-minute break coming up. I thought I'd have you for lunch."

A shiver of sensual delight went through her at his words. Straightening in her antique chair, she retorted, "Forget it. I'm not going to rush over to your office like some kind of bootycall delivery service. I might be your sex slave, but I do have some standards."

"I think you'll change your mind when you hear what I want to do to you…."

She listened to his low growl of a voice describing his intentions in graphic detail, and her hand went limp until the phone fell from her grasp and clattered to the floor. She snatched it up.

"I'll be right there," she said breathlessly. Clicking off, she pulled her new lingerie from the designer bag and tugged it on. Covering herself with the black puffy coat, that trailed to her ankles, she replaced her slippers with black stiletto boots and went outside, where a bodyguard held open her limousine door.

Bree's heart pounded as the chauffeur drove into the heart of St. Petersburg. She barely saw the elegant buildings lining the snowy streets and icy Neva River. All she could think about was what waited for her. *Who* waited for her.

The limo arrived at a sprawling eighteenth-century building. A bodyguard opened her door and said in heavily accented English, "This is office, miss."

She looked up and down the block. The structure seemed to stretch endlessly along the avenue. "Which one?"

The bodyguard looked at her. "All. Is Xendzov building."

"All of it?" Bree looked at the classically columned building in shock. It was one thing to theoretically know that Vladimir was rich. It was another to see this enormous building, an entire city block, and know it represented a mere fragment of his worldwide empire.

Swallowing nervously, she went into the foyer and took an elevator to the top floor. Down the hall, through a wall of glass, she saw men in suits packed around a conference table, some of them pounding the tabletop as they argued, while secretaries refilled their coffee cups and took notes.

Vladimir looked devastatingly powerful and ruthless, in a shirt and tie. And clearly, she wasn't the only woman to think so. She noticed how the secretaries walked a little more slowly and swayed their hips a little more around him. The beauty of Russian women was justly famous. Their skirts were short, their hair long, their stiletto heels high. They clearly knew their feminine power and were willing to sacrifice comfort in order to hold a man's attention.

Bree's confidence tumbled. If Vladimir was surrounded by women like this, why on earth had he sent for her? The sexy playfulness of her errand disappeared. What a laugh. It was like dialing out for a hamburger, when he was surrounded by steak!

He would laugh in her face when he got a good look at her in this stupid lingerie. Her cheeks burned and she started to turn around.

Their eyes met through the glass.

Spinning on her heel, Bree practically ran down the hallway. If she could just reach the elevator...

His hand gripped her upper arm, whirling her to face him. "Where are you going?"

She licked her lips, looking up at this broad-shouldered, powerful man standing in his own building, surrounded by his paid employees. Vladimir had rolled up his shirtsleeves, revealing sleekly muscled forearms laced with dark hair. His tie had been loosened around his thick neck, as if he'd been fighting corporate war all day.

She tried to pull away, but his grip was like iron. "I never should have come here," she said. "Haven't you humiliated me enough?"

Vladimir frowned, drawing closer. "What are you…?" People passed them in the hall, two men in suits and three women in tiny skirts, all looking at them with intense interest. Narrowing his eyes, he growled, "Come with me."

He pulled her into the nearest private office, closing the door behind them. She wrenched her arm away, blinking fast. Her eyes were stinging with unshed tears as she tossed her head. "You're out of your mind if you think…"

She gasped as, without a word, he roughly yanked open her oversized coat. He saw the lingerie, the white lace bustier, G-string panties and garter belt, and drew in a breath. He looked at her darkly.

"And *you* are out of your mind," he said in a low voice, "if you think I'm going to let you leave."

He ripped off her long coat, dropping it to the floor. Pushing her against the wall of the private office, he kissed her hard. Bree's body stiffened as his mouth plundered hers. She felt the soft, demanding steel of his lips against her own. Against her will, a moan came from the back of her throat, and her arms lifted to wrap around his neck.

His hands roamed over her body. He cupped her breasts, then undid her bustier in a single motion, dropping the white lace from her skin. Still kissing her passionately, he pushed her toward the desk, which he cleared with a sweep of his arm, knocking papers and computer topsy-turvy to the floor.

She could not resist. As he pressed her back against the desk, she relished the feeling of his weight. He kissed down her neck to her bare breasts, ravishing her body, and she panted, suddenly breathless with need. Her hands reached beneath his shirt to stroke his taut, hard chest.

Then she heard a noise at the door.

Dazed, Bree looked over and saw a man staring at them from the doorway. He said something in Russian, before Vladimir turned his head. The man's mouth snapped shut, his face red with the apparent effort of choking back his words. Turning, he left instantly, closing the door behind him.

But the damage was done. The man had seen her draped nearly naked across Vladimir's desk. Horrified, Bree said angrily, "That man's got some nerve, bursting into your office without warning!"

"This is his office—" Vladimir leaned back on the desk, tilting his head "—not mine."

"What?" she squeaked, sitting up.

"My office is on the other side of the building. Would have taken too long."

He leaned forward to kiss her, but she jerked back, nearly falling off the desk. "Are you crazy? I'm not going to fool around with you in someone else's office!"

"Why not?" he said lazily. "What does it matter? This building is mine. This office is mine. Just as you…"

She folded her arms over her naked breasts, glaring at him. "Just as I am?"

"Yes." Standing up, he tucked a tendril of hair behind her ear and said huskily, "Just as you are."

A pain went through her chest. His words were playful, but he was speaking a truth she'd been trying to conveniently forget: that Vladimir owned her. She was his property.

Bree's cheeks flooded with shame as she remembered the expression on the man's face when he'd seen Vladimir lying on top of her on the desk. He'd looked at her as if she were a prostitute. And glancing down at herself in only a G-string and garter belt, a sex-time delivery service, Bree felt a lump rise in her throat. Leaning down, she picked up the discarded bustier off the floor.

The smug masculine smile dropped from Vladimir's face. "What are you doing?"

She put on the long black coat, stuffing the bustier into the pocket. "Returning to my prison."

"Prison?" he repeated. "I have given you a palace. I've given you everything a woman could possibly desire."

"Right." She zipped the puffy coat all the way to her throat. As she turned away, she felt like crying.

Vladimir stopped her at the door. "Why are you so sad?"

The ache in her throat made it impossible to talk. She shook her head, unable to meet his eyes.

"You were—embarrassed?"

"Yes," she choked out.

"But why?" he demanded. "He is nothing. No one. Why do you care?"

Bree lifted her eyes. "Because I, too, am nothing," she whispered. "And no one."

He shook his head in exasperation. "I don't understand what you're talking about."

To you. I am nothing and no one to you. She turned her head. "I don't expect you to understand."

"Fine," he said coldly. "If you don't want to be here, go home."

She lifted her gaze hopefully. "Home to my sister?"

"Our home! Together!"

Her shoulders slumped. She stared down at her feet.

"There is no *together* at the palace," she said in a small voice. "There's just me. Alone."

"You know I am dealing with a complex merger, Breanna," he said tightly. "I have no time to—"

"I know." Her lips twisted. "I should just be grateful you show up in my bed in the middle of the night, right? Grateful you're so very, very good to me."

He ground his teeth, his eyes dark.

"I gave you my credit card. You should have bought out half the city by now. You should be enjoying yourself. You can buy whatever you wish—clothes, furs, shoes. And a ball gown. It is supposed to be fun."

"Fun," she muttered.

He scowled. "Is it not?"

"Shopping all by myself in a foreign city, as your bodyguards keep other people out of the store, and six different salesgirls try to convince me that a puce-colored burlap sack with ostrich feathers looks good on me…?" Bree shuddered. "No. It's not fun." She indicated the long black coat. "This is the sum total of my purchases."

He blinked. "The coat?"

"And the lingerie."

"Damn it, Bree, you aren't in Hawaii anymore. I told you to buy warm clothes."

"Who cares if I feel warm?" She glared at him. "I'm just your possession. My feelings don't matter."

He stared at her, and the air around them suddenly became electrified. "Of course they matter." He took a single step toward her. "Breanna—"

A knock sounded at the door. An older man poked his head in, an American with wire-rimmed glasses and anxious eyes. "Your Highness. Excuse me."

"What is it, Anderson?" Vladimir demanded.

The man looked at Bree and then cleared his throat. "We've reached an impasse, sir. Svenssen is demanding we retain every member of his company's staff."

"So?"

"Arctic Oil has a thousand employees we don't need. Drillers. Cafeteria workers in Siberia. Accountants and secretaries. Dead weight."

Dead weight. Bree's spine snapped straight. He would no doubt consider her and Josie *dead weight,* too, with their ten years of backbreaking, low-paying cleaning jobs. Every month, they'd experienced the painful uncertainty of never knowing if their jobs would last, or if they'd be able to pay their bills. Biting her lip, she glanced up and saw Vladimir watching her. His eyes narrowed.

"Tell Svenssen," he said slowly, "we'll find places for all his current employees. At their current pay level or better."

His employee gaped, aghast. "But, sir! Why?"

"Yes, why?" Bree echoed. She took a deep breath and gave him a trembling smile. "Don't tell me you've actually got a heart."

His lips abruptly twisted. "To the contrary." He turned back to Anderson. "I merely want to ensure that we're well staffed for future expansion."

"Expansion?" The man visibly exhaled in relief.

Vladimir lifted a dark eyebrow. "That should simplify your negotiations." Turning to Bree, he took her hand. "I will be unavailable for the rest of the day," he said softly.

"You will?" she breathed.

"But Prince Vladimir—"

He ignored the man. Pulling Bree from the office, he led her down the hall to the elevator. As he pushed the button, she looked at him, her heart in her throat.

"Where are we going?"

He tilted his head, giving her a boyish grin that took her breath away. "I'm going to show you my beautiful city."

His voice was casual. So why did she feel as if something had just changed between them, changed forever? She tried not to feel his strong, protective hand over her own, tried not to feel her own heart beating wildly. "But your merger is important. You said—"

"My people will manage. Let them earn their overpriced salaries."

"But why are you doing this?"

"I've realized something." Vladimir's eyes were ten shades of blue. "You belong to me."

She exhaled. "I know," she said dully. "You already said—"

"You belong to me." He cupped her cheek. "That means it's my job."

"What is?"

He looked intently into her eyes, and then smiled. "To take care of you."

Vladimir's mouth fell open as he stared at the beautiful angel who stood on a pedestal before him. Literally.

"Do you like it?" the angel said anxiously. "Do you approve?"

Bree was trying on her fourth designer ball gown, a strapless concoction in pale blue that revealed her elegant bare shoulders, the curve of her breasts and her slender waist above wide skirts of shot silk. She looked like a princess. Ethereal. Magical.

Intoxicating.

"I can't possibly let you buy this," the enchanted beauty said fretfully. "You won't let them tell me how much it costs, but I'm sure it's very expensive."

Vladimir lifted his hand, signaling to the five saleswomen who were hovering around them in the luxury designer atelier. "We will take it."

With a happy gasp, the salesgirls descended on Bree with sewing pins and measuring tape, to shape the couture gown perfectly to her body. Bree looked at them in dismay. But it was nothing compared to the sick expression he'd seen on her face when his COO had wanted to fire all the workers he called "dead weight."

Vladimir had lied. He wasn't planning an expansion. He'd just been unable to bear the emotions he'd seen on Bree's face: the anger, the powerlessness, the desperation. It reminded him how she'd spent ten years wasting her talents in minimum-wage jobs, because the man she'd trusted to protect her had left her to face all her enemies alone.

Now, she bit her pink, full lower lip. "I shouldn't let you do this."

"It's already decided." Rising to his feet, he felt glad once more that he'd decided to take the day off and spend it with her, leaving even the bodyguards behind. He put his hand on her shoulder. "You need a dress. I'm taking you to a very elegant ball for New Year's Eve."

Bree's dark-fringed hazel eyes went wide. "You are?"

"You will be," he said huskily, "the most beautiful woman there."

"I—I will?"

Her cheeks blushed in girlish confusion. Her charming innocence, at such odds with the wickedly seductive vixen she'd been when she'd shown up at his office building in lingerie hours before, made Vladimir want to kiss her.

So leaning forward, he did.

Her lips felt hot and velvety-soft. Her mouth parted for him, and he deepened the kiss. With a gasp, Bree started to wrap her arms around him.

Then she winced, pulling away. Rubbing her arm, she looked down at her skin. She'd been pricked by the needle of the salesgirl attempting to pin the waist of Bree's bodice.

Vladimir saw a small red dot of blood on Bree's skin, and was blinded by instant, brutal rage. He turned on the hapless girl and spoke harsh words in Russian.

The salesgirl choked back a sob and answered him with a flurry of begging and excuses. He stared at her, implacable as stone.

The salesgirl fell to her knees in front of Bree, holding the hem of the blue silk ball gown as she gazed up with imploring eyes.

Bree looked up at him uneasily. "What's she saying?"

"She's begging for mercy," Vladimir said coldly. "She's

saying she's the sole support of an aging mother and two-year-old son, and she's begging you to intervene with me, so I don't have her fired."

"You wouldn't do that!"

"I have just told her I will."

"What?" Bree gasped, staring at him. "No!"

"She hurt you," he said tightly.

"It wasn't her fault!" Bree tugged on the young woman's arms, forcing her to rise. "I'm the one who moved. And you're the one who kissed me! She never meant to stick me with her needle!"

"What does her intention matter? The pain for you was the same."

Bree was staring at him as if he were crazy. "Of course it matters! Why would I punish her for something that she didn't even mean to do? It was an accident!"

It was an accident. The memory of his brother's miserable, humbled voice on the phone ten years ago floated unbidden through Vladimir's mind. *Forgive me, Volodya. I'm sorry.*

"Don't have her fired. Don't!"

Bree's beautiful face came into focus. "Josie and I have been fired like this before." Her eyes were pleading as she clutched his arm. "You don't know what it's like, to always know that your boss or a single customer can just snap his fingers and take away your livelihood and your pride and your ability to feed your family." She swallowed, her heart-shaped face stricken. "Please don't do this."

Vladimir's lips parted. He didn't even realize he'd agreed to her request until he saw Bree's beautiful face light up with happiness. He dimly heard the grateful sobs of the Russian girl, but as Bree threw her arms around him, he felt only her. Saw only her.

"Thank you," she whispered. She drew back, tears sparkling in her eyes. "And thank you for that huge tip you gave her as an apology. I never expected that." A smile lifted Bree's trembling lips. "I'm starting to think you might have a heart, after all."

Huge tip? Looking down, Vladimir saw that his wallet was indeed open in his hand, and was now considerably lighter. The salesgirl was holding a wad of rubles, weeping with joy as she shared the unexpected largesse with the others.

"It was kind of you, to care for her."

His cheeks burned as he turned back to Bree. "I don't give a damn about her."

"But—"

He cut in. "I did it for you."

She took a deep breath.

"That's why I know you have a heart," she whispered.

And Vladimir knew she was right. Because in this moment, his heart was beating erratically, misfiring, racing.

Taking her hand in his own, he pulled her down from the pedestal. "I just want you to be happy," he said roughly. He didn't know how to manage this reckless, restless yearning he felt every time he looked into her beautiful face, every time he touched her. He looked down at her hand, nestled so trustingly in his. "I want to give you a gift."

"You already did."

"Tipping a salesgirl doesn't count."

She looked down at the exquisite blue ball gown. "You're buying me this dress."

"I want to do something for you," he growled. "Something you actually care about. Anything."

Her eyes went wide with dawning, desperate hope.

"Set me free," she choked out.

Let Bree go? He couldn't. *Wouldn't.* After ten years, he'd found her again. What were the chances of them walking into the same poker game in Hawaii? Surely fate had placed her there for a reason?

She'd brought sunlight and warmth into his life. But if he

let her go, she might leave. He couldn't take that risk. Not now. She meant too much.

Folding his arms, he scowled. "You lost fair and square."

"But this is what I want, more than anything—"

"*No,* Breanna." He set his jaw. "Something else."

Crushing disappointment filled her eyes. She looked down. "My birthday is in a few days. Let me fly back to the States and spend it with my sister. I'm worried about her…."

"Josie is fine. My men left her in Seattle, as she requested. She has money. She is fine."

"So why haven't I been able to reach her phone?" She swallowed. "I've always taken care of her…."

"She's a grown woman," he said, irritated. "And you coddle her like a child."

Her eyes flashed. "Coddle!"

"Yes, *coddle.* She will never grow up until you allow her to make her own choices, and live with the consequences!"

Bree stiffened. "Like you did, you mean—cheating your brother out of the company?"

He glared at her. "He chose to leave, rather than accept my leadership. It made him strong. Strong enough to be my rival!"

"Your enemy, you mean!"

Controlling himself, Vladimir exhaled. "Breanna, I don't want to fight."

She licked her lips, then shook her head. "I don't, either. But I have a reason to protect Josie. I told you, there are men who want to hurt us…."

With a harsh word and a clap of his hands, Vladimir scattered the salesgirls, leaving him alone with Bree in the dressing room. Coming closer, he put his hands on her shoulders and said in a low voice, "Those men won't be bothering you."

She blinked. "They won't?"

"My people tracked them down. One of the men was already dead, unfortunately." Vladimir gave a grim smile. "But the other two will never bother you or Josie again."

Her eyes were huge. "What did you do?" she whispered. "Tell me you didn't…break anything."

Vladimir narrowed his eyes. "I wanted to. But I respected your request. I paid them off. Also, my investigator gathered enough evidence to have them both thrown in prison for the rest of their lives. If they ever cross your path again, even accidentally, that information will go to the local police. And they will die in jail." He looked at her blank face, suddenly uncertain. "Is that satisfactory?"

"Satisfactory?" She took a deep breath, then with a sob, threw her arms around him. "Thank you," she whispered. "We're free!"

He looked down at her, wiping the tears off her cheek gently with his thumb. "I'll never let anyone hurt you or your sister, Breanna. Ever again."

Her lower lip wobbled. "Thank you."

Seeing her reaction, he wanted to do more. He heard himself say, "And I'll have my men look around Seattle. See if they can track Josie down."

"Okay," she sniffled.

"Do you have any idea where she might be?"

She shook her head. "We used to say that when we got back to the Mainland, if we had money, we'd start our own bed-and-breakfast, or a small hotel." Her cheeks flushed. "But the truth is, that's my dream, not hers. She wants to go to college."

"Don't worry. I'll find her." Pulling his phone out of his pocket, he turned away. He was stopped by Bree's small voice.

"People call you ruthless. But it's not true."

Slowly, he turned to face her.

Bree's hazel eyes were luminous, piercing his soul. "When we met, I thought you'd changed completely from the man I loved. But you're still the same, aren't you?" she whispered. "The other man—he's just the mask you wear."

Vladimir's forehead broke out in a cold sweat. He felt bare

beneath the spotlight. "You're wrong," he said roughly. "I *am* ruthless. Selfish, even cruel. Don't believe otherwise."

She shook her head. "You're afraid people will take advantage, so you hide your good heart—"

"Good heart?" He grabbed her shoulders, looking down at her fiercely. "I am selfish to the bone. I will never put someone else's interests ahead of my own. I cannot *love,* Bree. That ability is no longer in me. It died a long time ago."

"But—"

"Would a good man keep you prisoner against your will?"

She lifted her gaze. Her hazel eyes were suddenly troubled, opaque, full of shadows.

"No," she whispered.

No. That one word caused an unexpected wrench inside him. As the two of them stood in the huge private dressing room of the designer atelier, her expression became impassive—her poker face. He wondered what she was thinking. In this moment, when he felt so strangely vulnerable, his insight into her soul suddenly disappeared.

"I'm not a good man, Bree," he said in a low voice. To prove it further—to both of them—he lowered his mouth to hers, kissed her hard enough to bruise. She kissed him back with fierce passion, but he felt her withholding something he wanted. Something he needed.

Unzipping her blue ball gown, Vladimir kissed the bare skin of her neck. Her hair smelled like sunlight and passion fruit, like vanilla and the ocean, like endless summer.

Her strapless silk bodice fell, revealing her white bustier. They were surrounded by mirrors on three sides, and as he saw endless reflections of him touching her, he felt so hard he wanted to take her roughly, against the wall. So he did. As the dress fell to the hardwood floors, he unzipped his pants and lifted her, shoving her roughly against the mirrored wall. Barely pausing to sheath himself in a condom, he thrust inside her. Wrapping her legs around his hips tightly, she clutched his shoulders as he filled her, slamming her against the wall. Five thrusts and she was moaning. Ten thrusts and she clutched her fingertips into his shoulders as her body tightened, her back arching. Fifteen thrusts and she screamed with pleasure in cries that matched his own.

Afterwards, for an instant, panting and sweaty, he just held her, his eyes closed. Then slowly he released her legs, letting her body slide down his. The passion had been hotter than ever.

But he knew something had changed between them. An unbridgeable gap.

"Get dressed," he said. "We have dinner reservations."

"Fine," she said dully, not meeting his eyes.

He zipped up his pants, and she put on her new clothes, the slim-fitting black pants, sheer black top over a black camisole, and black leather motorcycle jacket he'd bought for her earlier at a department store on Nevsky Prospekt. All afternoon, he'd insisted on buying everything he saw in her size, anything she could possibly want to wear for the rest of her life, for any season and any event.

Compensating, he thought. Though he knew she couldn't be bought.

Even if he'd bought her.

"Before dinner," he said brightly, despising the false cheer in his voice, "I wish to buy you something truly special. A fur coat. White mink, perhaps, or Barguzin sable—"

Bree shook her head. "No, thanks."

"Russian furs are the best in the world."

Her eyes were cold. "I don't want a fur."

He set his jaw. "You're pouting."

"No." She looked away. "I just used to have a dog when I was a kid," she mumbled. "I loved that dog. We used to explore the forest all summer long. He had a soul. He was my friend."

She was talking about her dog? Vladimir exhaled. He'd been bracing for her anger, since the only thing she really wanted was the one thing he wouldn't, couldn't, give her. Relieved, he lifted his hand and lightly traced the bare skin of her collarbone. "I still don't understand the connection."

"I'll put it in simple terms." Pulling away from him, she folded her arms. "No fur."

"As you wish," he whispered, taking her hand in his own. He felt her shiver. He looked at her. Her expression was completely unreadable. He sighed. "Come."

Leaving the dressing room, he went out to meet with the salesgirl and finish the details of the order, arranging for the hand-stitched ball gown to be delivered the next day. Vladimir took Bree outside, where his bodyguard awaited them beside his bulletproof limo.

"Where are we going?"

"You'll see."

"I'm tired of shopping."

"You'll like this."

Twenty minutes later the limo pulled to a stop. Helping her out himself, Vladimir led her past two security guards into a tiny, high-ceilinged shop in the belle epoque style, with gilded walls and colors like a cloisonné Easter egg. Everything about the jewelry store bespoke elegance, taste and most of all money.

"What are we doing here?" Bree scowled. "I thought we had dinner reservations!"

He gave her a teasing smile. "This won't take long."

A short, plump man with wire-rimmed glasses and a short white beard, wearing an old-fashioned pin-striped suit with a vest, came eagerly from behind one of the glass cases. "Welcome, welcome, Your Highness," he said in Russian.

"Speak in English so she'll understand."

"Of course, Prince Vladimir." Tenting his hands, the jeweler turned to Bree and switched to accented English. "My lady. You are here for a necklace, yes? For the New Year's Eve ball at the ancient palace of the Romanov tsarina?"

Bree glanced up at Vladimir. "Um. Yes?"

He smiled back at her, feeling a warm glow at the thought

of spoiling her. "I wish to buy you a little something to wear with the ball gown."

"I don't need it."

"*Need* has nothing to do with it." He lifted a dark eyebrow. "Surely you won't deny me the small pleasure?"

Her scowl deepened. "No. How could I?"

He ignored her insinuation. "Surely," he said teasingly, "you will not tell me that diamonds remind you of a former pet? That they possibly have a *soul?*"

She looked down at the floor.

"No," she whispered. "A diamond is just a cold, heartless stone." Vladimir frowned. She suddenly seemed to recall she was speaking to the CEO of Xendzov Mining, one of the largest diamond producers in the world. Flashing him a wry smile, she amended, "But they are pretty. I'll give you that."

"So you'll let me buy you something."

"Don't you have a closetful of diamonds back home? I'm surprised you don't use them like rocks to decorate your garden."

"My company produces raw diamonds. We sell them wholesale. The fine art of polishing them into exquisite jewelry is not our specialty." He lifted his hands to indicate the little jewel box of a shop. "This is the best jewelry store in the world."

"Really? In the world?"

He gave her a sly smile. "Well, the best in St. Petersburg. Which means it is the best in Russia. Which means, naturally, that it is the best in the world."

Staring at him for a moment, she shook her head with a sigh. "All right." Her tone was resigned. "Since it seems I have no choice."

Vladimir had truly expected this to be a quick stop en route to dinner at the best restaurant in the city. He'd assumed Bree would quickly select one of the most expensive necklaces in the store: the looped rope of diamonds, the diadem of sapphires, the emerald choker that cost the equivalent of nine hundred thousand dollars. But an hour later, she still hadn't found a necklace she wanted.

"Six million rubles?" she said now, staring down incredulously at the ropes of diamonds patiently displayed by the portly jeweler. "How much is that in dollars?"

He told her, and her jaw dropped. Then she burst into laughter. "What a waste!" She glanced at Vladimir. "I won't let you spend your money that way. Might as well set it on fire."

He didn't have nearly the same patience as the jeweler. "Money isn't a problem," he said tightly. "I have more than I could spend in a lifetime."

"Lucky you."

"I mean it. After you make a certain amount, money is just a way to keep score."

"You could always donate the money to a charity, you know. If you hate it so much," she said tartly.

He gave a low laugh. "I didn't say I hate it. If nothing else, it gives me the opportunity to drape you in diamonds."

"Against my will."

"I know you will love them. All women do."

"*All* women?"

That hadn't come out right. "It's a gift, Bree. From me to you."

"It's a chain." She reached out a hand and touched the glittering diamond rope resting on the glass case, then said bitterly, "Diamond shackles for an honored slave." She looked up at the jeweler. "No offense."

"None taken, my lady."

She looked at Vladimir. "Thanks for wanting to buy me a gift. But I don't need a chain to remind me of my position."

Vladimir felt irritated. He'd wanted to buy something that would please her, to distract her from the one thing he would not give: her freedom. "I am trying to make you happy."

"I can't be bought!"

"You already were," he said coldly.

Bree gave an intake of breath, and her eyes dropped. "Fine. Buy it for me, then. Because you're right. You can do whatever you want."

Her voice dripped with icy, repressed fury.

This was turning into a disaster. Vladimir's intention in bringing her here had been to make her cry out in delight, clapping her hands as she threw her arms around him in joy. But it seemed no cries of joy would be forthcoming.

He forced his clenched hands to relax. "I think we're done." Turning away from the jewelry case empty-handed, leaving the disappointed jeweler behind them, Vladimir put his hand on her back. It was an olive branch, an attempt to salvage the evening. "Fine. No diamonds. But you will enjoy dinner."

"Yes," she said. "Since you are telling me to enjoy it, I must."

They were very late for their reservation. But when they finally arrived at the restaurant, adjacent to an exclusive hotel on the Nevsky Prospekt, he had the satisfaction of seeing Bree's mouth fall open.

Art-nouveau-style stained glass gleamed in a wall of windows. Shadowy balconies and discreet curtained booths overlooked the center parquet floor, filled with tables covered with crisp white linen. White lights edged the second-floor balustrade, and tapering candles graced the tables with flickering light as uniformed waiters glided among the planted palm trees, serving rich, powerful guests.

The maître d' immediately recognized Vladimir. "Your Highness!" Clapping his hands, he bowed with a flourish and escorted them to the best table.

"Everyone is looking at us," Bree muttered as they walked across the gleaming parquet.

Relieved she was finally talking to him again, Vladimir reached over to take her hand in his. "They're looking at you."

As they were seated, Bree's cheeks were pink, her eyes glowing in the flickering light of the candles and warmth of the high-ceilinged restaurant. Soaring above them on the ceiling were nineteenth-century frescoes, country scenes of the aristocracy at play.

When the waiter came, Vladimir ordered a short glass of vodka, then turned to Bree. "What would you like to drink?"

She tilted her head. "The same."

"It's vodka."

"I'm not scared."

"Are you sure?" He lifted a dark eyebrow. "You don't strike me as much of a drinker."

She shrugged. "I can handle myself."

Her bravado was provocative. He looked at her beautiful, impassive face, at the way her dark eyelashes brushed her pale skin, at the way her stubborn chin lifted from her long, graceful neck. He wondered what she would say if she knew what he was thinking.

"Your Highness?" the waiter said in Russian.

Vladimir turned back to him and gave the order. After the man left, Bree said abruptly, "Where did you learn Russian? It wasn't at school."

"How do you know?"

"I don't," she admitted. "But I know you and your brother grew up on the same land that now belongs to Josie—or will, in three years." She tilted her head. "It's funny we never met. Both of us growing up in the same state."

"That land was in our family for four generations. A thousand miles from anything. You know." He drummed his fingertips on the table, looking for the waiter with the vodka. "So we kept to ourselves. My father spoke Russian with us. He was proud of our history. He homeschooled us. In the long winters, we read Pushkin, Tolstoy." Vladimir's lips twisted. "It was my mother who made sure our home had food and wood. The land is our legacy. In our blood."

"Why did your mother sell it to my father?"

His body tightened. "I was desperate for money to start

our business. Kasimir absolutely refused to sell. He'd made some deathbed promise to our father. But I knew this was the only way."

"You had nothing else to sell? You couldn't take a loan?"

"Mining equipment is expensive. There is no guarantee of success. Banks offered to loan us a pitiful amount—not nearly enough to have the outfit I wanted. We'd already sold the last item of value our family possessed—a necklace that belonged to my great-grandmother—to help fund college in St. Petersburg. *Spasiba,*" he said to the waiter, who'd just placed their drinks on the table. Reaching for his vodka, he continued, "So I talked to my mother. Alone. And convinced her to sell."

"Behind your brother's back?" Bree's eyes widened. "No wonder he hates you."

Knocking back his head, Vladimir took a deep drink and felt the welcoming burn down his throat. "I knew what I was doing."

"Really." Bree's cheeks were pink, but her troubled gaze danced in the flickering candlelight. "Do you know what you're doing now?"

"Now?" He set his glass back on the table with a clunk. "I am trying to make you happy."

Her eyes were impassive. "Without letting me go."

Reaching across the table, he took her hand in his larger one. "I have no intention of letting you go. Ever."

"Why?" She swallowed, then glanced right and left at all the well-dressed people around them. "You could have any woman you want. Even the gorgeous secretaries at your office…"

"But I want only the best." His hand tightened over hers. "And the best is you."

She stared at him, then shook her head. "I can see how you twist women's hearts around your little finger."

"There's only one woman I want." He looked at her beautiful, stricken face over the flickering candle. "I've never forgotten you, Breanna. Or stopped wanting you."

He felt her hand tremble before she wrenched it from his grasp. She reached wildly for her untouched glass of vodka and, tilting back her head, drank the whole thing down in a single gulp.

That gulp ended with a coughing fit. Reaching around her, he patted her on the back. Her face was red when she finally managed a deep breath, wheezing as she quipped, "See? I know how to handle vodka. No problem."

Somewhat relieved by her deliberate change of subject, Vladimir laughed, his eyes lingering on her beautiful face. He'd said too much. And yet it was oddly exhilarating. The adrenaline rush of emotional honesty put skydiving to shame, he thought. About time he tried it.

The waiter returned to take their order, and Vladimir requested a dinner that included Astrakhan beluga caviar and oysters, vodka-marinated salmon and black risotto, steak in a cream sauce and a selection of salads, breads and cheeses. Bree shook her head in disbelief when the exotic food started arriving at the table, but ninety minutes later, as she gracefully dropped the linen napkin across her mostly empty plate, she was sighing with satisfied pleasure.

"You," she proclaimed, "are a genius."

He gave her a crooked grin, ridiculously pleased by her praise. "I've come here a few times, so I knew what to order."

"That was perfect." She rose to her feet. "If you'll excuse me."

"Of course." Vladimir watched her disappear down the hall toward the ladies' room, and realized he was sitting alone at the best table in the most famous restaurant in St. Petersburg, grinning to himself like a fool. Feeling sheepish, he looked around him.

His gaze fell on a face he recognized, of a man sitting alone in a booth on the other side of the restaurant. This particular man in this particular place was so unexpected that it took him thirty seconds to even place him, though they'd spent many hours across the same poker table over the past two months. The Hale Ka'nani hotel manager, Greg Hudson. What was he doing in St. Petersburg?

Perhaps the man was on vacation. In Russia. In winter. Telling himself he didn't care, Vladimir turned his chair away, so the man was out of his sight.

Today was the best day Vladimir had had in a long time. Even though leaving subordinates to handle the merger so he could spend time with his mistress was reckless, irresponsible, foolish. Even though he'd likely lose a fortune retaining all the employees of Arctic Oil. Even so.

Instead of feeling guilty, he kept smiling to himself as he recalled how Bree's eyes sparkled when she was angry at him. The way her body had felt, pressed against his in the mirrored dressing room of the boutique. She was fire and ice. She was life itself.

"Hawaii has changed you completely." His doctor had been shocked by the test results that morning, when Vladimir stopped on the way to the office. "You've recuperated from your injury better than I ever dreamed. Even your blood pressure is improved. What have you been doing? Yoga? Eating bean sprouts? Whatever it is, clean living is making you healthy. Keep it up!"

With a laugh, Vladimir glanced down at his empty vodka glass and half-eaten plate of beef rib eye drenched in sauce. Clean living? No. *Good* living. It wasn't yoga and bean sprouts. It was laughter, good company and lots of sex.

It was Breanna.

Vladimir shifted impatiently in his chair, craning his head to look past the waiters and candlelit tables toward the wood-paneled hallway. His lips rose in unconscious pleasure when he saw Bree coming back down the hall.

Then a dark figure came out of the shadows to accost her. Seeing Greg Hudson, Vladimir rose to his feet. Bree looked surprised, then angry, as the man spoke to her. Vladimir clenched his jaw as he strode rapidly toward them. Hudson's eyes went wide when he saw him coming. Turning, he ran out of the restaurant.

"What did he say to you?" Vladimir demanded.

Bree turned with a carefully blank look on her face. Her poker face, he thought, but he could see her lips trembling. Her gaze dropped. "Nothing."

"Tell me."

"He…" She licked her lips. "He told me he's in St. Petersburg to collect a debt, and happened to see me." Her eyes carefully remained on the gleaming parquet floor. "He said he's going to be very rich in a few days, and he would pay a lot of money to be my next lover. He wondered if there was some kind of waiting list."

Anger made Vladimir's vision red. He started to turn, his hands clenched. "I will kill him."

"No. Please," Bree whispered. She put her hand on his arm. "Just take me home."

People in the restaurant were staring at them, whispering behind their hands. "But we already ordered dessert," he said tightly. "Chocolate cake. Your favorite."

"I just want to go." Her cheeks were red. "And forget this day ever happened."

Forget this day ever happened? The wonderful day he'd spent with her—the hours he'd spent watching her laugh, telling her the truth, buying her things, trying so hard to please her—as he'd never tried to please any woman? "I don't want to forget."

She looked away. "I do."

Shoulders stiff, Vladimir went across the restaurant and tossed thirty thousand rubles on their table. Getting her leather coat, he wrapped it around her shivering shoulders and led her out into the cold, dark night. As his chauffeur drove their limousine home, Vladimir looked out at the snowy streets of

St. Petersburg. It had been the best day of his life, but it had ended with Bree in tears.

He wanted to blame the fat little hotel manager. But he knew there was one person at fault for the way she'd been so crudely insulted as a woman who could be bought and sold at any man's will.

Vladimir himself.

CHAPTER EIGHT

THE next night, Bree paused as she got ready for the New Year's Eve ball. She looked wanly out the tall curved window of their bedroom.

The wintry Gulf of Finland on the Baltic Sea looked nothing like Hawaii's warm turquoise waters. It was even worse than Alaska's frigid sea. Even in the weak, short hours of daylight, the Russian waves were choppy and gray. But the sun had set long ago, and the world was dark. The black, icy water here could suck the life out of you within seconds if you were dumb enough to fall into it.

Kind of like falling in love with a man who would neither love you back nor set you free.

Bree closed her eyes. Yesterday, the workaholic tyrant had been neither workaholic nor a tyrant, playing hooky from work to entertain her. Letting people keep their jobs in his merger. Tipping that saleswoman at the boutique. Getting rid of the men who'd threatened Bree and her little sister. And more.

I've never forgotten you, Breanna. She would never forget the stark vulnerability in his blue eyes. *Or stopped wanting you.*

Bree trembled with emotion, remembering. Thank heaven she'd been able to cover her reaction by gulping that nasty-tasting vodka. She should probably be grateful for Greg Hudson, too. His words had brought her back to reality with a snap.

Bleakly, she opened her eyes. She was alone in their bedroom, with one leg propped up on the bed, pulling on sheer black stockings as she got ready for the New Year's Eve ball. Her beautiful haute-couture princess gown was on the bed, waiting to go over her new black lace bra, panties and garter belt. Vladimir had bought out every expensive store in the city. "I am trying to make you happy," he'd said. But she couldn't be bought that way. Only two things could make her happy, and they were the very things he would not or could not give her. Freedom. Love.

I am selfish to the bone. I will never put someone else's interests ahead of my own.

She couldn't let herself fall for him. She'd loved him once, and it had nearly killed her. She'd lost everything.

Never again. Unless they were equals, loving him was only a different kind of bondage. Especially since, in the eyes of the world, Bree was nothing more than his whore.

Hadn't meeting with her ex-boss proved that?

"Well, well, what a pleasant surprise," Greg Hudson had drawled, stepping into her path in the hallway last night. "If it isn't the poker-playing maid herself."

She'd been shocked to see her former boss's beady eyes and sweaty face. Instead of a tropical shirt, he was dressed in the required jacket and tie, probably borrowed from the restaurant, since they didn't fit his lumpy body.

"Mr. H-Hudson," she'd stammered. "What are you doing in St. Petersburg?"

"Call me Greg." He came closer, crowding her space in the darkened hallway. "I'm here to collect a big debt. Thought I'd celebrate at the best restaurant in town."

"You left the Hale Ka'nani?"

His expression darkened. "I got fired. The hotel's owner found out I took a bribe." He tilted his head, his eyes sly. "Didn't you ever wonder why I hired you and that sister of yours?"

Bree sucked in her breath as all her old worries came back. "Someone bribed you to hire us? Who?"

Leaning forward, he wheezed, "Even he didn't think I'd be as successful as I was. In a few days, I'll be paid, and given a huge bonus. I'll be rich enough to pay you directly, for services rendered. I want to be on your waiting list. Name your price." He'd stroked her upper arm, and she'd caught the scent of whiskey, heavy and sour, on his breath before he saw Vladimir and turned away. "Come to me when Xendzov is done with you."

Bree's face burned as she remembered the humiliation of that moment. She'd been completely unprepared for it. And even more unprepared for the suspicion that had slithered into her soul ever since.

Who would have paid Greg Hudson to hire the Dalton sisters at the Honolulu resort?

All night Bree had stared up at the bedroom ceiling in the dark gray light, going through countless scenarios in her mind. It could have been one of her father's old enemies. Or…it could have been Vladimir himself. To make her his prisoner forever, to enjoy at his will.

I've never forgotten you, Breanna. Or stopped wanting you.

She sighed. But that didn't make sense, either. He'd been surprised to see her. She'd seen it in his face, in his body. He'd had no idea she was in Hawaii.

So who?

Vladimir had been an extraordinarily tender lover last night, but even as he'd made her body shake and gasp with pleasure, her soul had been haunted by the question. Finally, at breakfast that morning, before he'd left for work, he'd stated, "I'm sorry you were insulted last night. It will never happen again."

"Thank you," she'd murmured, though they both knew it was a lie. There was no way he could prevent that. If she wasn't insulted to her face, she'd still be able to see it in people's eyes.

She was his possession. Nothing more, nothing less.

Now, staring out at the dark, wintry night, Bree felt an ache in her throat. She finished pulling on her stockings, attaching them to her garter belt. If only she had someone to talk to about this. If only she could talk to Josie...

Vladimir's voice was husky behind her. "Are you ready?"

With an intake of breath, Bree turned to face him. He stood in the doorway, half in silhouette. He looked broad shouldered and impossibly handsome in a dark, exquisitely cut tuxedo. She tried not to notice. "Have you found Josie?"

"Josie?" he repeated absently. He came toward her, his blue eyes gleaming as they traced slowly down her nearly naked body in the black lace. "Forget the ball. Let's stay home for New Year's Eve."

She felt his gaze against her skin the same as if he'd stroked her with his fingers. Her breath caught in her throat, and she trembled with desire and something more—something that went straight to her heart. She wrapped her arms around herself. "My sister. Have you found her yet?"

He blinked, then his eyes lifted to hers. "Not yet. My investigator did trace her back to Hawaii."

"Hawaii!" Something was wrong. Bree could feel it. "Why would she go back?"

He shrugged. "Perhaps she forgot something at your old apartment."

"Spending every penny she owns, just to go back for some old sweater or something?"

Vladimir pressed his lips together. Bree saw him hesitate, then reluctantly say, "Apparently she was trying to get the police to take an interest in your case. But they laughed at her, both in Seattle and Honolulu." He looked at Bree sideways. "They thought our wager sounded like a lovers' game between consenting adults."

"Right." She had a sick feeling in the pit of her stomach. "So where is she now?"

He shook his head. "The trail went cold."

Josie was missing? Bree opened her mouth, then stopped.

Telling him her fears would do no good. She feared it would only set off another tirade from him about how Josie was a grown woman and that Bree should allow her sister to face her own consequences.

And for all she knew, he was right. For ten years, her fears had been on overdrive where Josie was concerned. How was Bree supposed to know when it was rational to worry and when it was not?

"We'll find her." Vladimir was watching her. "Don't worry."

"I'm not," she lied.

"Good." Reaching into his pocket, he held out a flat, black velvet box. "This is for you."

She flinched when she saw the jewelry box. He'd known she hated the diamond necklace, but *he'd bought it anyway.* The chain of her captivity.

"You went back and bought it," she said dully.

He glanced at the blue silk ball gown draped across their bed. "It goes with your dress."

Ice filled her heart, rushing through her like a frozen sea. In spite of all appearances to the contrary yesterday, he didn't care about her feelings. He wanted to dress her to appear well. Like a show dog on display. "You are too kind."

A smile curved his sensual mouth, as if he knew exactly what she was thinking. "Open it."

"You."

"Don't you want to see it?"

"No." Closing her eyes, she lifted her hair. "Just do it," she choked out.

Bree heard the box snap open. She felt the warmth of his body as he moved to stand behind her. She felt a heavy weight against the bare skin beneath her collarbone. It was surprisingly heavy. Frowning, she opened her eyes.

A simple gold chain hung around her neck, with an enormous green pendant wrapped in gold wire. Shocked, she touched the olive-green jewel, the size of a robin's egg. "What's this?"

"It's a peridot," he said quietly. "Carved from a meteorite that fell to Siberia in 1749. It once belonged to my great-grandmother."

Bree's mouth fell open. "Your—"

"The pendant was a wedding gift from my great-grandfather, before he sent her and their baby son into exile. To Alaska."

Bree felt the roughness of the peridot beneath her fingertips. The sharp crystalline edges had been worn smooth by time.

"We sold this necklace to a collector, to help pay for college." He ran a finger along the chain. "It took me years, and a large fortune, to get it back." He put his hand over the stone, near her heart, and lifted his gaze. "And now it is yours."

Bree gasped. Feeling the weight of the necklace and the warmth of his hand, she looked down at the stone. In the shadowy bedroom, the facets flashed fire, green like the heart's blood of a dragon. "I...I can't possibly keep this."

"Too late." Vladimir's handsome face was expressionless.

"But it's too valuable." She swallowed as her fingers stroked the gold chain against her skin. Their hands touched, and she breathed, "Not just the worth of the stone, but the value to your family..."

Drawing back, he said harshly, "It is yours." He turned away. "Finish getting ready. I will wait for you downstairs."

She suddenly felt like crying. "Wait!"

He stopped, his back stiff, his hands clenched into fists.

"This should belong to someone you care about," she whispered. "Someone...someone special."

He didn't turn around.

"You are special to me, Breanna," he said in a low voice. "You always have been."

She couldn't just let him leave. Not when he'd proven to her, once and for all, that she was more than a paid concubine. As he headed for the door, she rushed across the room, catching him from behind. Wrapping her arms around his body, she pressed her cheek against his back. "Thank you."

Slowly he turned around in her arms.

"I need you to know. You are more than just my possession." His darkly handsome face was stark. Vulnerable. "You are…"

"What?" Her throat ached.

"My lover."

Unable to speak, she nodded.

Wiping her cheek with his thumb, he said in a low voice, "Come. Get dressed. We don't want to be late." He gave her a crooked smile. "I don't want to miss kissing you at midnight."

Seeing that boyish, vulnerable smile, her heart twisted. "No. We don't want to miss that."

He picked up her silk ball gown from the bed, and she stepped into it. As he pulled it up around her, she felt his fingers brush against her spine. She looked back at him with an intake of breath. His gaze was hungry, his eyes dark as the midnight sea. She should expect more than just a kiss to celebrate the New Year.

She wasn't his girlfriend. She wasn't his wife. But perhaps…

Her fingertips ran softly over the necklace that had once belonged to a Russian princess, and a green stone that two hundred and fifty years ago had landed in Siberia from the farthest reaches of space. Perhaps he did care for her, after all.

Could that caring ever turn to something more? To love?

I cannot love. She heard the echo of his hard voice. *That ability is no longer in me. It died a long time ago.*

As Vladimir finished zipping up the ball gown, he turned her to face him. Brushing tendrils of hair from her face, he looked down at her with electric blue eyes. "Are you ready?"

Looking up at his handsome face, Bree tried not to feel anything. But her heart slammed against her ribs.

His forehead furrowed. "Bree?"

She turned away with a lump in her throat. "I, um, need some lipstick." Going to the mirror, she made her lips bright

Chanel red. Lifting the silk hem of her gown, she stepped into her expensive shoes with sparkling crystals decorating the four-inch heels, and took a deep breath. "Ready."

Downstairs in the foyer, Vladimir took a sharply tailored black coat from the closet, wearing it over his tuxedo. Then he removed a black hanging bag from the closet. He unzipped it. In dismay, Bree saw white fur.

He noted her expression. "Don't worry. It's fake."

Dubiously, she reached out and stroked the soft white fur. "It seems real."

"Well." His lips curved in amusement. "It's *very* expensive. Twice the price of the real thing." Lifting the white fur coat from the bag, he wrapped it around her bare shoulders. "I can't have you getting cold, *angel moy,*" he said softly.

"What does that mean?"

"My angel."

She bit her lip, faltering. "I'm nobody's angel."

He smiled. Pulling her close by the lapels of the white faux fur, he looked down at her. His blue eyes crinkled. "Wrong."

Bree's heart squeezed so hard and tight she couldn't breathe. Still smiling, he held out his arm and led her outside into the cold, frosty night.

The limousine whisked them to a small town on the edge of St. Petersburg, to a palace that had once belonged to a Romanov tsarina three hundred years before. Bree's eyes widened as the road curved and she got her first view of it. With a gasp, she rolled down the window for a better look.

Beneath the frosted winter moon, she saw the palace that had once been a summer getaway for the Russian royal family. The elegant structure, wide and sprawling, looked like a wedding cake, decked with snow. The limo drove up the avenue, past a wide white lawn lit up by flickering torches.

The limo stopped, and a valet in breeches and an eighteenth-century wig opened Bree's door and helped her out. Feeling the shock of cold, bracing air on her face, she looked around in awe. She touched the green peridot against her skin, beneath her white fur. Standing in this courtyard, she could almost imagine herself as the princess of an ancient, magical land of eternal winter.

She could almost imagine she was a Russian prince's bride.

His bride. As Vladimir took her hand in his own, smiling at her with so much warmth she barely even needed a coat, she could not stop herself from wondering, just for an instant, what it would be like to be his wife. To be the woman he loved, the mother of his children.

"Are you still cold?" he murmured as they passed the bowing doormen.

She shook her head.

"But you're shivering."

"I'm just happy," she whispered.

Stopping inside the palace doors, he pulled her into his arms. Kissing the top of her hair, he looked down at her with a smile.

"At last," he said softly. "I have what I wanted."

Searching his gaze, Bree sucked in her breath. That smile. She couldn't look away. It was so open. So…young. He looked exactly like the young man she'd first fallen in love with, so long ago.

The man she'd never stopped loving.

As he took her hand to lead her down the elegant hallway, Bree nearly stumbled in her sparkling high-heeled shoes.

She was in love with him.

She could no longer deny it, even to herself.

Vladimir took her into the ballroom, and Bree barely noticed the exquisite, lavishly decorated space, the gilded walls or the crystal chandeliers high above. She barely spoke when he introduced her to acquaintances. As he led her out onto the dance floor, she didn't see all the gorgeous people all around them.

She saw only him. She felt only his arms around her, and the rapid thrum of her own heart.

She loved him. It was foolish. It was wrong. But she could no more stop herself than she could stop breathing. She loved him.

For hours, they danced together. They drank champagne. They ate. They danced some more. For Bree, it all flashed by in a moment. In his arms, she lived a lifetime in every precious minute. The regular laws of time were suspended. Hours sped by in seconds.

Suddenly, as they were dancing, the music stopped. Lifting her cheek from his chest in surprise, Bree saw it was nearly midnight.

Vladimir looked down at her as they stood unmoving on the dance floor, and as the last seconds of the year counted down, for Bree it was as if time not only became suspended, but was reversed. His gaze locked with hers, and ten years disappeared.

She was eighteen and he was twenty-five. They were in each other's arms. The world was new. Brand-new.

He cupped her face. "Breanna…"

Cheers went up around them in the ballroom as she heard the last seconds of the year counted down in a jumble of languages, German, French, Chinese, Spanish, English, and Russian loudest of all.

"Pyat…"

"Cheteeri…"

"Tree…"

Lowering his head, Vladimir said huskily, "Let's start the New Year right…"

"Dva…"

"Ahdeen…"

His lips pressed against hers, smooth and rough, hard and sweet. He kissed her, and fire flashed not just through her body, but her soul.

"S'novem godem!" Raucous cheers and the sound of horns and singing revels exploded across the ballroom. "Happy New Year!"

When Vladimir finally pulled away from their embrace,

Bree stared up at him, her heart in her throat. She swayed, nearly falling over without his arms around her.

"S'novem godem," he murmured, cupping her cheek tenderly. "Happy New Year, *angel moy*."

She looked up at him.

"I love you," she choked out.

He stared at her, his eyes wide.

All around them, people were dancing to the music of the orchestra, laughing, drinking champagne, kissing each other. But Vladimir was completely still.

Tears filled Bree's eyes as she gave him a trembling smile. "Even when I hated you, I loved you," she whispered. "When I made the wager in Hawaii to be yours forever, part of me must have been willing to lose that bet, or I never would have made it." She licked her lips. "You have always been the only man for me. Always."

He did not answer. His face was pale, his blue eyes as frozen as a glacier.

A chill of fear sneaked into her soul.

"And what I need to know is…" She bit her lip, then lifted her gaze to his. "Can you ever love me?"

Vladimir's eyes suddenly narrowed. He cleared his throat.

"Excuse me," he said shortly. He walked past her, leaving her alone on the dance floor.

Mouth agape, Bree turned and stared after him in amazement. Her cheeks went hot as she noticed exquisitely dressed Russians and other wealthy, beautiful people staring at her with open curiosity. Embarrassed, she walked off the dance floor.

She'd never felt so alone. Or so stupid.

She lifted her hand to the necklace, to the heavy weight of the peridot against her bare skin.

He cares for me, she repeated to herself silently. *He cares.*

But even that beautiful jewel seemed small consolation, considering that she'd just confessed her love for him, and he'd left her without a word.

Maybe he was called away on urgent business. At midnight. On New Year's Eve. She clawed back tendrils of her long blond hair. Why had she told him she loved him, and worse, asked if he could ever love her back? She knew he couldn't! He'd told her that straight-out, from the start!

Oh, God. She covered her face with her hands. She was an idiot.

Maybe when he came back, she could give a hearty laugh, as if it had all been a joke. She could tell him she'd been pretending to have Stockholm syndrome or something. She could be persuasive with her lies, as she'd been long ago. She could turn off her soul and disconnect from her heart. She knew how.

But…

She pulled her hand away. *She didn't want to.* She was tired of bluffing. She didn't want to be that con artist anymore. Ever again.

And sometimes telling the truth, showing her cards, would mean she lost the game.

She gave a ragged laugh. She'd never expected the cost to be this high. Snatching a flute of champagne from a passing waiter, she tried to sip it nonchalantly, as if it was quite enjoyable to be standing on the edge of the dance floor in a blue Cinderella gown, alone in a crowd of strangers. But as minutes passed, she suddenly wondered if Vladimir was even coming back. For all she knew, he'd already jumped into the limo and was heading for the airport.

Why not? He'd abandoned her before. Without a single word. She squeezed her eyes shut. *Please don't leave.*

A prickle went up her spine as she felt someone come up behind her. Vladimir, at last! In a rush of relief, she turned.

But it wasn't Vladimir. A different man stood before her, slightly younger, slightly thinner, but with the same hard blue eyes—only filled with cold, malevolent ruthlessness.

"Kasimir?" Bree whispered. "Kasimir Xendzov?"

"Having a good time?" he replied coldly. Before she could

answer, he grabbed her arm and pulled her away from the crowd, into a private alcove. She stared at him. She'd met him only once before, in Alaska, the Christmas night he'd burst in upon them, desperate to tell his brother the truth about Bree's con. He'd been twenty-three then, barely more than a boy. Now...

Bree shivered. Now he was a man—the type of man you would never want to meet in a dark alley. She yanked her arm away from his grasp. "What do you want? If you've come to find your brother—"

"I haven't come to see my brother." Kasimir gave her a cold smile. "I came for you."

"Me?" she breathed.

"It's about...your sister."

"Josie?" An icy chill went down her spine. "What about her?"

He came closer, invading her personal space. She instinctively backed away. He straightened, and his eyes glittered. "I've married her."

"What?" Bree gasped.

He gave her a cold, ruthless smile. "Your little sister has become my dear, dear wife."

"I don't believe you!"

For answer, he pulled something from his pocket and held it out to her on his palm. Josie's cell phone. Bree snatched it up. There could be no doubt. She saw the colorful rhinestones that her sister had glued to the back in the shape of a rainbow.

"I asked her to marry me some time ago," Kasimir said, "and she refused. Until you disappeared. Then she came back. She offered to do anything, *anything,* if I would only save you from my evil brother. Marriage was my price."

"But why would you want to marry her?" Then suddenly Bree knew, and her heart dropped to the floor. "The trust," she said dully. "You want her land."

"It's not *hers,*" he said tightly. "It's been in my family for a hundred years. It never should have been sold. We've fought for it, died for it—" Catching himself, he relaxed his clenched hands. "So. The land will be mine in three days, when the banks reopen. After that, I can either divorce her quickly with a nice settlement, or…"

"Or?"

His eyes met hers coldly. "Or I can seduce her, make her fall in love with me and destroy her pitiful little heart. I can force her to be my wife forever, and you will never see her again. It is your choice."

Bree flinched, even as her heart pounded with fear. "How do I know this isn't all some lie? It might just be some sick joke, some game in the battle between you and your brother—"

Taking the cell phone away from her, he dialed a number, then pressed the phone back against Bree's ear. She heard her little sister's voice.

"Hello?"

Bree gripped the phone. "Josie," she gasped. "Where are you?"

"I'm so sorry, Bree," her sister whispered. "The poker game was all my fault. I was trying to save you. That's why I married him…."

"But where are you?" Bree cried.

Kasimir yanked the phone away. As he disconnected the call, Bree went for him, her hands outstretched. He pushed her away easily, tucking the phone in his tuxedo jacket pocket.

"Tell me where she is," she cried. "Or—or I'll kill you!"

"You're scaring me," he drawled.

"Then…" Bree had already threatened to kill him. What could be more frightening than that? She lifted her chin furiously. "I'll tell Vladimir!"

Kasimir's expression was cold. "Go. Tell him."

She was flabbergasted at his casual tone. "But he will destroy you!"

"He's tried to destroy me for years," he said scornfully, "and

I only grow stronger." He moved closer. "And you are wrong, Miss Dalton," he said softly, "if you think his desire for you will make him sacrifice anything for you or your family. He cares for you because you please him in bed, and he values that pleasure. But given the choice between helping you or himself, he will not hesitate."

Was Kasimir right? She licked her lips, barely hearing the music from the nearby ballroom. With a deep breath, she lifted her hand to her necklace. She felt its rough weight around her throat.

"Vladimir cares for me," she whispered.

"Because he gave you my great-grandmother's necklace?" His brother lifted a dark eyebrow. "He sold that once, you know. And he will sell you, if it ever gives him any advantage."

"You're wrong."

"Try him and see," Kasimir suggested silkily. "Go to him. Explain how Josie agreed to marry me and give me every acre of the land. He will say her predicament is her own fault, for being foolish enough to seek me as her ally. Vladimir is not a man who excuses mistakes. He punishes them." His brother narrowed his eyes. "He will not lift a finger to save her."

Bree trembled in her blue silk ball gown. Was it true?

Vladimir had cut Kasimir out of his life completely, cheating him out of hundreds of millions of dollars, just because of a few angry, drunken words to a reporter. He'd forced Bree to live as his mistress even when she'd begged him for her freedom—all because of a one-card wager. "You made the bet," he'd said. "Now you will honor it." Thinking of how he'd just abandoned her on the dance floor when she'd told him something he apparently didn't want to hear—that she loved him— Bree's heart lifted to her throat.

Would he treat Josie any more mercifully?

"She will never grow up," she remembered his hard voice saying. "She will always be helpless and weak, unless you allow her to face the consequences of her own actions."

"What do you want me to do?" she whispered.

Kasimir's eyes glittered. "You will help take back what should have been mine." Pulling an envelope from his pocket, he handed it to her. "Make him sign this."

"What is it?"

"A deed that transfers control of his company to me."

Bree stared down at the paper. "I hereby renounce all shares in Xendzov Mining OAO," it read, "giving them freely and in perpetuity to my brother...."

She looked up, openmouthed. "He will never sign it."

"You are a clever girl, with a flair for trickery and deceit." Kasimir tilted his head. "For your sister's sake, you will make him sign. Even if it causes you a small twinge of grief." He walked slowly around her. "Your lies caused *me* a great deal of grief ten years ago. I am glad to finally see you and my brother suffer—together. I could not have it planned better."

Bree's heart gave a sickening thud.

"It was you," she breathed. "You're the one who arranged for us to be taken to Hawaii. You're the one who bribed Greg Hudson to hire us."

Kasimir smiled. "My brother was stuck there, bored out of his mind, attending the same poker game each week. I knew he had a weakness for you. I hoped seeing you would cause him pain." Kasimir snorted. "Instead, you created an opportunity for justice I never could have imagined. You insinuated yourself into his life. Like a disease."

"Even if his signature is obtained through trickery," she said desperately, "it will never stand up in court."

"Then you have nothing to worry about, do you?" he said coolly. "Bring the signed document to my house in Marrakech within three days."

"And if I fail?"

He looked straight into her eyes, like an enemy looking over the barrel of a gun. "Then you'll never see your sister again. She'll disappear into the Sahara. And be mine. Forever."

Bree shook her head with a weak laugh. "You're joking."

"I am a madman. Ask my brother. He knows." Kasimir looked at her blue silk ball gown. "Your sister was frantic about you. She came to me, begging for help. She was willing to do anything to save you, even sacrifice her own soul." His lips twisted into a sneer. "And for the last two hours I've watched you, drinking champagne, dancing in his arms, giggling like a whore." She flinched as he growled, "So much for Josie's *sacrifice*."

Bree sucked in her breath, lifting her gaze. "You like her, don't you?" she said slowly. "I can see it in your eyes. I can hear it in your voice. You don't want to hurt her."

Kasimir glared at her, gritting his teeth. "What I *want* is revenge. And I will have it." Turning away, he said over his shoulder coldly, "You have three days."

CHAPTER NINE

WITH a low curse, Vladimir shoved the short fat man out of the palace, into the dark, deserted garden.

"What the hell are you doing in St. Petersburg?" he demanded.

"I'm allowed to visit here, if I want. You don't own this city, Xendzov," Greg Hudson brayed in response, shivering in his badly fitting tuxedo. "It doesn't *belong* to you!"

"Wrong," Vladimir replied coldly, shoving him again. Moments before, in the middle of Bree's innocent, tearful declaration, he'd seen Greg Hudson skulking near the buffet table. Vladimir had been overwhelmed by Bree's three simple words. He hadn't known how to react to them.

Seeing Greg Hudson, he'd known exactly what to do.

Fury had filled him at the sight of the man who'd insulted her, offering money to be *on her list*. He'd dragged him out of the ballroom, wanting to knock him to the ground and kick him repeatedly in his soft belly until he learned to respect women. Especially Vladimir's woman. "You will leave this city and never come back."

Hudson quivered like a rabbit. "Think you're something big, do you, Mr. Hoity-Toity Prince? You have no idea how you've been played!"

Ignoring him, Vladimir lifted his fist. "Were you following her?"

The man flinched. "No! I swear! I just happened to be in

town—" he looked up slyly "—to see your brother. The other prince."

Vladimir slowly lowered his fist. "You know Kasimir?"

"He owes me money."

"For what?"

The man looked smug.

Grabbing him with one hand, Vladimir lifted his other fist and thundered, "For what?"

"He offered me a lot of money to hire those Dalton girls. And a bonus if I could arrange for you to meet the older one. By accident."

Vladimir's body turned hot, then cold. His hand tightened on the man's lapel.

"If you ever disrespect Miss Dalton again," he said evenly, "if you so much as mention her name or look at her picture in the newspaper, you will regret it for the rest of your short life." He gave him a hard stare. "Do we understand each other?"

"Y-yes," the man stammered. "I never meant any harm."

Vladimir let him go, and Hudson fell back into the snow. Leaping up again with a gasp, he fled into the night, slipping on ice in his haste, leaping over a snowdrift as he called wildly for his driver.

Relaxing his clenched fists, Vladimir exhaled.

Slowly, he turned back toward the palace. But he felt numb, as frozen as if he'd fallen asleep in the white snow. He looked out at the fields in the moonlight. So soft. So beautiful. So mysterious.

So treacherous.

Breanna's beautiful face appeared in his mind. Was it possible…could it be that meeting her had been more than a co-incidence? That it had been a plan cooked up by Bree and Kasimir, to finally get their revenge for his treatment of them ten years ago?

Was he a gullible fool falling for the same woman's lies—twice?

If Kasimir hired Hudson, Vladimir told himself harshly, *Bree didn't know.*

Or did she? Against his will, a gray shadow of suspicion filled his soul.

As he entered the ballroom and walked through the crowds, his feet dragged. He had no idea what to do. What to say to her.

"I love you," Bree had said. His heart beat with the rhythm of her words. "And what I need to know is, can you ever love me?"

How could she love him? Bree was too smart for that. He'd warned her that he would never love her. Told her it was impossible. He wanted to make her happy, yes. He'd bought her clothes, spent time with her, gotten rid of the men who'd threatened her and Josie. But what had that cost him, really? Nothing.

No matter what she seemed to think, there was no shred of goodness in Vladimir's soul. He would never risk or sacrifice anything that truly mattered.

All he had to offer was sex and money—and though Bree seemed to very much enjoy the sex, she didn't care about money. So what could she possibly see to love in his black soul?

He'd kept her against her will. Stolen her freedom for his own selfish pleasure. She should hate him. Instead, she'd offered him everything. Not just her body, but her soul. Her warmth, her tenderness and adoration, her honest heart.

If it really was honest.

No. He wouldn't think that. It was Kasimir who'd arranged their meeting, not Bree. But why? What could possibly be his goal?

Vladimir pushed through the crowd, his pulse throbbing in his throat. He had to find Breanna. He hungered to feel her in his arms, to know she was real. To look into her eyes and see that she wasn't—couldn't be—allied with his brother against him. Vladimir needed her. That was as good as love, wasn't it?

She deserves a man who can love her back with a whole, trusting heart. The thought whispered unbidden in his mind.

Not the careless, shallow affection you can give her, the shadowy half love of a scarred, selfish soul.

She's mine, he told the voice angrily.

So you'll keep her as your prisoner forever, taking her body every night without ever returning her love? Until you see the adoration in her eyes fade to anger, then bewildered hurt, and finally dull, numb despair?

Vladimir closed his eyes. He couldn't let that happen. Not to Breanna. He couldn't feed on her youth and energy, like a vampire draining love and life from her body.

If he couldn't love her, he had to let her go.

But damn it. *How could he?*

He sucked in his breath when he saw her across the ballroom, like a modern-day Grace Kelly, willowy, blonde, impossibly beautiful in her strapless, pale blue ball gown. But her shoulders drooped. She stood alone by the dance floor. Shame shot through him. He could only imagine what she was thinking, after the way he'd left her.

Grabbing two flutes of champagne, he came up behind her, then touched her on the shoulder. "Breanna..."

She jumped, turning to face him. Her eyes were wide, her cheeks pale. "Oh. It's you."

"Who were you expecting?"

She tried to smile, but her expression looked all wrong. "A handsome prince."

He wondered if she'd seen that little weasel Greg Hudson, in spite of his effort to get the man out of the ballroom quickly. "Did someone...bother you?"

"Bother me?" She tossed her head with forced bravado. "You know I can take care of myself."

"Tell me what's wrong," he said quietly.

She took a deep breath, then lifted stricken eyes to his. "You just...ran away so fast from me on the dance floor, I thought you'd be halfway to Berlin by now."

Ah. He suddenly knew why she was upset. "Um. Right."

The collar of his shirt felt tight. "Sorry I left like that. I was... thirsty." That sounded ridiculous. He pushed a champagne flute into her hand. "I got you something to drink."

Vladimir waited for her forehead to crease in disbelief, for her to demand why he'd really run off the instant she'd told him she loved him. For her to challenge and goad him into telling her the truth.

But she didn't. Her fingers closed around the stem of the crystal flute, but her thoughts seemed a million miles away.

"Hey." He touched her cheek lightly, and she lifted startled eyes. "Are you angry with me?"

Her lips parted, then she shook her head.

"No," she whispered. "Why would I be?"

Putting the flute to her lips, she tilted back her head and gulped down the expensive champagne like water.

For a long, awkward moment, Vladimir just stood there, pretending nothing was wrong. They didn't speak or touch or even look at each other as, all around them, people drunkenly, joyously celebrated the New Year. Finally, Vladimir could bear it no longer.

"I don't blame you for being angry." Taking the empty glass from her hand, he deposited it on the tray of a passing waiter, along with his own untouched champagne. He took her hand in his. "But Bree," he said slowly. "You have to know how I feel...."

With a sudden intake of breath, she looked up, her hazel eyes luminous. "It's my sister. She needs my help."

Her *sister?* He'd been raking himself over the coals, hating himself for hurting her, and all this time she'd been thinking about that hapless sister of hers?

He exhaled. "You need to stop worrying about her. My men will soon track her down. In the meantime, she's a full-grown woman. Treating her like a child, following her around to fix her slightest problem, you'll make her believe she's useless and incompetent. And she will be."

"But what if, this time, she really needs my help?" Bree's beautiful face grew paler. She searched his gaze with an intensity he didn't understand. "What if she's done something—something that might destroy her life forever—and I'm the only one who can save her?"

Irritated, he set his jaw. "Like you saved her from the hundred thousand dollars she lost at the poker game? When you risked yourself, offering your body to strangers, to save her from the consequences of her actions?"

Her voice was very small. "Yes."

Narrowing his eyes, Vladimir shook his head. "If she didn't learn from that, she never will."

"But—"

"There is no *but*," he said harshly. "She is twenty-two years old. She must learn to make her own choices, and live with them."

Bree's shoulders were rigid. She fell silent, turning away as she wiped her eyes. On the dance floor, people were still swaying to the music, toasting the New Year with champagne and kisses. But somehow, he wasn't quite sure how, the mood between him and Bree had utterly changed. And not for the better.

"I'm sorry," she said in a low voice, not looking at him. "I can't just abandon the people I love the instant they make a mistake. I'm not *you*," she said tightly.

Feeling the sting she no doubt intended, he said in a low voice, "My brother made his own choice to get out of the company."

"Because you made him feel worthless for a single mistake. When all he did was tell you the truth about yours."

"Falling in love with a woman who was deceiving me," he said, watching her.

"Yes," she whispered. She shook her head. "No wonder he hates you."

"He intends to destroy me," Vladimir said shortly. "But not if I ruin him first."

Her expression became bleak. "Neither of you will ever give up, will you? No matter who gets hurt."

There was no way she was working with Kasimir, Vladimir thought. *No way.* He exhaled. "Forget it." He gave her a crooked smile. "Sibling relationships should be my last topic of advice to anyone, clearly. Or relationships of any kind. What do I know about loving anyone?"

But his attempt at an olive branch failed miserably. Her eyes looked sadder still. She glanced down. "I'm tired."

"All right," he said in a low voice. "Let's go home."

As soon as we get back to the palace, I'll seduce her, he told himself. They would get everything sorted out in bed.

But once they arrived there, Bree was even more distant, colder than he'd ever seen her. Colder than he'd ever imagined she could be.

She didn't fight with him. She just withdrew. She moved away when he tried to pull her in his arms. "I want to go to bed."

"Great," he murmured. "I'll come with you."

"No." She practically ran up the stairs, then looked down from the top landing, a vision in a blue gown, like a princess. Like a queen. "Tonight, I sleep alone."

Her voice wasn't defiant. It wasn't even angry. It was inexpressibly weary.

He frowned, suddenly puzzled. None of this made sense, but he knew one thing: somehow, some way, he had screwed up. "Bree," he murmured, "what you said to me, back on the dance floor—"

"Forget about it." She cut him off and drew a deep breath, her hands tightening at her sides. "It doesn't matter. Not anymore."

But it did matter. He knew that from the way his heart seemed about to explode in his chest. But he couldn't let himself feel this. He couldn't…

Anger rushed through him, and he grabbed at it with both

hands. Climbing the stairs, he faced her. "You can't keep me out of our bed, Bree. Not tonight. Not ever."

She looked at him coldly.

"Try it, then, and see what happens, Your *Highness*."

Turning on her heel, she left him. And if Vladimir had had any hope that he might be able to warm her up, as he climbed naked into bed beside her ten minutes later, those hopes were soon dashed. Bree lay on the other side of the large bed, pretending to be asleep, creating a distance between them so clear that the space between them on the mattress might have been filled with rabid guard dogs and rusty barbed wire.

Their romantic, magical night hadn't exactly gone as planned. Lying in bed, Vladimir tucked his hands behind his head and stared at the shadows on the ceiling. The reason for her coldness was all too clear. She'd said she loved him, and he hadn't said it back.

But he couldn't say it. He didn't feel it. He didn't *want* to feel it.

There. There it was.

He didn't want to love her.

He'd done it once. He'd given her everything, believed in her, defied his brother and all the world for her sake. And he'd only proved himself a fool. He would never let himself feel that way again. He would never give his whole heart to anyone.

Especially not Breanna. No matter how much he admired her, or how much he cared. He wouldn't let her have the power to crush his heart ever again.

But as a gray dawn broke over the first day of the New Year, Vladimir looked down at Breanna beside him in bed, listening to her steady, even breathing as she slept. He saw trails of dried tears on her skin.

Tomorrow was her birthday, he remembered. She would be twenty-nine years old. She'd saved herself for him for ten years. She'd been brave enough to give herself to him completely, holding nothing back.

I love you. Her words haunted him. *Even when I hated you, I loved you. You have always been the only man for me. And what I need to know is—can you ever love me?*

Instinctively, his hands pulled her sleeping body closer. He breathed in the vanilla-and-lavender scent of her hair.

Could he continue to use her beautiful body in bed, keeping her prisoner to his pleasure, watching as her love for him soon turned to hatred, then numb despair?

He had no choice.

Sitting up, Vladimir leaned his head against the headboard, feeling bleak.

If he couldn't love her, he had to let her go.

Bree woke up with a gasp of panic and fear.

Seeing she was alone in bed, she fell back against the pillow with a sob. Within three days, she would have to betray someone she loved. Who would it be?

Josie?

Vladimir?

She felt sick with grief and guilt and fury. Numbly showering and getting dressed, she went down downstairs, where she spoke in terse monosyllables when Vladimir greeted her, wishing her a cheery Happy New Year. She kept her distance from the man she loved, sitting as far as possible from him at the long table as they ate the elaborate holiday breakfast prepared by the chef. She stopped all of Vladimir's attempts at conversation and just generally made herself unpleasant. But having him close, looking into his handsome, trusting face, was like poison to her.

For some reason, he was bending over backward to try to be nice to her, which made her feel even worse. But by late afternoon, her rudeness had managed to push him to the limit. With a muttered, inaudible curse, he stomped off to work in his home office.

And Bree exhaled, her heart pounding and blood roaring through her ears.

What should she do?

She had to save her little sister. There was no question. Whatever it took to save Josie, she would do. Immediately.

Except…

Betray the man she loved? Could she really steal Vladimir's company, his life's work, the only thing he truly cared about—and give it to his brother?

Bree's mind whirled back and forth in such panic that her body trembled and her knees were weak beneath the strain.

The clock was ticking.

"You have three days," Kasimir Xendzov had told her. Less than that now. She looked at the clock. Her hands shook, desperate to take action. But what action?

She could contact the police. True, they were in Russia and Josie was…anywhere in the world. But they could contact Interpol, the American Embassy, something!

But while Bree was trawling through layers of international bureaucracy and jurisdictional red tape, Josie would be gone, never to resurface.

I can seduce her, make her fall in love with me and destroy her pitiful little heart, Prince Kasimir had said. *I can force her to be my wife forever, and you will never see her again.*

Bree paced across the morning room, stopping to claw her hand through her tangled hair. She felt like crying. She didn't know what to do.

Tell Vladimir everything, her heart begged. *Throw yourself on his mercy and ask for help.*

Right, she thought with a lump in her throat. Since Vladimir was such a merciful man.

But still, three times that afternoon, she went down the hallway of the palace to the door of his study. Three times she raised her hand to knock, wanting to confess everything. But each time, something stopped her.

His own words.

She is twenty-two years old, he'd said harshly. *She must learn to make her own choices, and live with them.*

And each time, Bree put her hand down without knocking. What if Vladimir said Josie had brought this on herself, by seeking Kasimir's help?

If Bree told him everything, and he refused to help her, she would lose her chance to get him to sign Kasimir's document. And all hope for Josie would be gone. Her baby sister would be left terrified and alone, somewhere in the Sahara. Bree would never see her again.

Vladimir doesn't even love you, a voice argued.

But I love him. She swallowed. *He deserves my loyalty.*

And what about your little sister, whom you've always protected? What does she deserve?

Bree covered her face with her hands. She was stuck, frozen, equally unable to betray either of them. And time was running out.

If only fate could make the decision for her…

"Breanna." She jumped when she heard Vladimir's voice behind her. "I'm sorry if I've neglected you today." He put his arms around her, nuzzling her neck. His voice was humble, as if he thought he was to blame for their estrangement. "I should work tonight. Paperwork for the new merger has piled up, and it all needs my signature by tomorrow."

Twisting her head, Bree looked back at him, her heart breaking. He'd just told her exactly how to get Kasimir's document signed. Was it fate?

"But let it wait until tomorrow." Smiling down at her, he kissed the top of her head. "Shall we have dinner?"

But by the end of the night, Vladimir's smile had turned to bewilderment. They slept in the same bed, a million miles apart. When Bree woke up alone the next morning, January 2, she realized two things.

Today was her birthday. She was twenty-nine years old.

And the whole meaning of her life came down to this one choice. Which of the people she loved would she betray?

Sitting up in bed, she looked at the gilded clock over the marble fireplace. Over half the time since Kasimir's ultimatum was gone, and she'd done nothing. She'd neither tried to trick Vladimir into signing the dreadful contract, nor confessed the truth and begged him for help. For the past day and a half, since midnight on New Year's Eve, she'd always felt one breath away from crying. So she'd pushed him away, to keep him from seeing into her soul. In response to Vladimir's innocent question yesterday, asking what she wanted for her birthday, she had answered so rudely that she blushed to remember it now.

She couldn't tell him what she really wanted for her birthday.

Freedom from this terrible choice.

Bree's knees trembled as she slowly climbed out of bed and fell blearily into the shower. She got dressed in a black button-down shirt and dark jeans. She combed out her long, wet hair. She pulled it back in a severe ponytail.

Cold, she told herself as she slowly pulled on her black stiletto boots. *My heart is cold. I am an iceberg. I feel nothing.*

Tucking the document Kasimir had given her beneath her black shirt, she went down the wide, sweeping stairs in Vladimir's eighteenth-century palace, as if she were going to her death.

After so many gray, snowy days, brilliant sunshine was pouring in through the tall windows, leaving patterns of golden light on the marble floor. She'd been happy here, she realized. In spite of everything. She'd loved him.

Looking back now, Bree saw it had been enough. They'd been happy. Why hadn't she appreciated that happiness? Why had she fretted, worried, groused about Vladimir's one major flaw—that he didn't want her to ever leave him? What kind of stupid flaw was that? Why hadn't she just fallen to her knees in gratitude for all the blessings she'd had—so unappreciated then, and now so swiftly gone?

Creeping softly to the open door of his study, she peeked inside. Empty. Holding her breath, keeping her mind absolutely blank, she swiftly walked inside and stuck the page in the middle of the pile of papers she'd seen him working through yesterday. She would distract him today, and if luck was on her side, he would sign it without reading it. She felt confident he wouldn't suspect her.

He trusted her now.

As Bree left the study on shaking legs, she hated herself with every beat of her heart.

Perhaps having his company stolen wouldn't hurt him too badly, she tried to tell herself. Hadn't Vladimir insinuated that it had become a burden? "Money is just a way to keep score," he'd said. Perhaps he would someday understand, and forgive her.

But even now, Bree knew she was lying to herself. Even if he was able to accept losing Xendzov Mining—even if he started over and built a successful new company, as Kasimir had—she was making herself his enemy for the rest of his life. The fact that she'd done it to once again save her sister would not gain her any points, either. He would despise her. Forever. Everything between them, every good memory, would be lost.

Bree walked heavily down the gilded hall, past the arched windows. She heard the sharp tap of her stiletto boots against the marble floor. Brilliant January sunlight reflected off the white snow and sparkling Gulf of Finland. She looked out the windows, and saw sun as warm as his touch. Sky as blue as his eyes.

Suddenly even walking felt like too much of an effort. She stopped, staring at the floor, her heart in her throat.

"Breanna. You're awake."

Blinking fast, she looked up. Vladimir was coming down the hall toward her, looking impossibly handsome in a white button-down shirt and black slacks. An ache filled her throat as she looked into the perfect face of the only man she'd ever loved. The man she was about to lose forever.

"I have something for you. A birthday present."

Her voice was hoarse. "You shouldn't have."

He gave her a crooked grin. "You can't already hate it. You don't even know what it is yet."

The warmth of Vladimir's grin lit up his whole face, making his soul shine through his eyes, making him look like the boy she'd known. Like everything she'd ever wanted.

Swallowing, she looked down at her stiletto boots. "I'm just not in much of a party mood."

He took her hand. She felt his palm against hers, felt his fingers brush against her own as he pulled her gently down the hall. "Come see."

He led her into a high-ceilinged room centered around a glossy black grand piano. The conservatory had a wall of windows overlooking the sea. Antique Louis XIV chairs flanked the marble fireplace, and expensive paintings covered the walls, along with shelves of first-edition books.

"I know you said you didn't want a fur coat," Vladimir said. "But if you're going to live in St. Petersburg, you need some Russian fur to keep you warm…."

Bree saw a lumpy white fur stole on the pale blue couch beside the window. With an intake of breath, she cried, "Vladimir, I told you—"

He gave her a crooked half grin. "Just go look."

Hesitantly, Bree walked toward the blue couch. She got closer, and the lump of white fur suddenly moved, causing her to jump back with a surprised little squeak. From the pile of fur, a shaggy white head lifted.

She saw black eyes, a pink tongue and a wagging tail. Vladimir lifted the puppy into her arms.

"She's an Ovcharka. A Russian sheepdog." Lowering his head, he kissed her softly. "Happy birthday, Breanna."

With a little bark, the white puppy wiggled her tiny furry

body with joy, warm and soft in Bree's arms. Cuddling the dog close, she looked up at Vladimir's smiling face, and felt a bullet pierce her throat.

She burst into tears.

"Bree, what is it?" He bent over her, his handsome face astonished and worried. "You seemed sad about the dog you'd lost long ago, so I thought… But I see I've made a mistake." He clawed back his dark hair. "It was a stupid idea."

"No," she choked out. She tried to wipe her tears off her cheek with her shoulder. "It was a wonderful idea," she whispered. "The best in the world."

"Then why are you crying?" he said, bewildered.

Trying to choke back her tears, she buried her face in the dog's soft, warm fur. "Because I love her." Looking up, she whispered, with her heart in her throat, "And I love you."

He grinned, clearly relieved. "What will you name her?"

Heartbreak. She stared at him for a long moment, then looked at the windows. "Snowy."

"Snowy, huh? Did you put a lot of thought into that?" But the teasing grin slid from his face when she gave him no answering smile. He cleared his throat. "Well, I have one more surprise for you. But you'll have to wait until dinner to get it."

As the day wore on, Bree's heart broke a little more with each hour. They played with the puppy, then had a delicious late lunch with champagne. Afterward, the palace staff rolled in a giant, lilac-frosted cake on a cart.

"Chocolate cake," Vladimir said happily. "With lavender frosting."

"Is this my big surprise?" she asked, dreading further kindness.

"No. And don't ask me about it. You won't get it out of me. Even if you use your feminine wiles."

He said it as if he were rather hoping she would try. It had been two nights since they'd made love. It felt like a lifetime.

The heat in his eyes made her cheeks go hot, along with the rest of her body. Trembling, she pretended not to notice.

The servants sang Happy Birthday to her in cheerful, slightly off-key English, led by Vladimir's low, smooth baritone. He lit the two wax candles on the cake—one shaped like a 2, the other a 9.

He nudged her with his shoulder. "Make a wish."

Leaning toward the flickering candles, Bree closed her eyes, wondering what she'd done to deserve this fresh hell. And knowing it wasn't what she'd done, but what she was about to do.

She took a deep breath, her wish a silent prayer: *I wish I didn't have to hurt you.*

She blew out the candles, and everyone applauded.

As the staff departed, after giving Bree their well wishes in a mixture of English and Russian, Vladimir took her in his arms.

"Do you want to know about your other gift?" he said softly.

She gulped. "I thought you weren't going to tell me."

"If you kiss me, I might change my mind."

But she backed away. "I'm not really in a kissing mood, either," she mumbled.

From the corner of her eye, she saw the stiffness of his posture, and felt his hurt. "Very well," he said finally. "It is your special day. You don't have to do anything you don't want to do."

He paused. She didn't move. His hands tightened at his sides.

"So I'll just tell you what the big surprise is, shall I?" he said. "I've bought you a hotel. The Hale Ka'nani Resort."

She looked up with a gasp. "What?"

"You dreamed of someday running a small hotel." He gave her a crooked smile. "I bought you one."

"But the Hale Ka'nani isn't *small!* It must have cost millions of dollars!"

"Two hundred million, actually."

"What?"

"Don't worry." His lips lifted in a smile. "I got a good deal."

"Are you out of your mind?"

"It's an investment. In you."

Tears filled her eyes. "Why would you do something so stupid?"

"Because…" he said softly, reaching a hand toward her cheek "…with your brilliant strategic mind, Bree, I've always known you were born to rule an empire."

Trembling, fighting tears, she stumbled back from his touch.

"I need to take Snowy for a walk," she blurted out, and, picking up the puppy, she fled to the white, snow-covered lawn outside. Once there, Bree dawdled, taking as long as she could, until her cheeks and nose felt numb from the cold and even the puppy was whimpering to go back to the warmth inside. It was past dusk when she finally returned to the conservatory, her feet heavy, her heart full of dread.

To her surprise, the room was empty. The puppy flopped down on a rug near the warm fire, and Bree frowned. "Where is he?" she said aloud.

The puppy answered with a stretch and a yawn, clearly intending to have a long winter's nap.

Bree went down the hall, passing various rooms. Then she saw Vladimir. In the study. At his desk. Signing papers.

Shock and horror went through her like lightning.

"What are you doing?" she breathed.

"There you are." His voice was cold, and he didn't bother to look up. He seemed distant—and how could she blame him? "I will join you for a late dinner after I finish this."

He was signing the papers by rote, with rapid speed, as if his mind was on something else. She saw Kasimir's contract peeking out beneath the next paper. "Stop!"

"I got your message loud and clear, Bree." He pushed the

top paper aside. "You don't want anything from me. You can't even bear to look at me—"

As he reached, unseeing, for Kasimir's contract, Bree suddenly knew.

She couldn't let him sign it. She couldn't betray him.

She *couldn't*.

With a choked gasp, Bree flung herself across his study and blocked him the only way she knew how. Shoving his chair back, she threw her leg over him, straddling him, separating him physically from his desk. Tangling her hands in his hair, pressing her body against his, she leaned forward and kissed him.

At first he froze. For one dreadful instant she thought he would push her away. Then a sound like a low sigh came from the back of his throat, and his powerful arms wrapped around her. His lips melted roughly against hers.

The pen in his hand dropped to the floor. The pile of papers on his desk was forgotten.

Holding her against his chest, Vladimir rose and, in a savage movement, swept the papers off his desk. Pressing her back against the polished oak, he looked down at her with eyes so full of emotion that her heart caught in her throat.

"Now, Bree," he said hoarsely, as he lowered his mouth to hers. "I need you now."

CHAPTER TEN

VLADIMIR had never felt such fire.

Bree had never initiated lovemaking before. The heat of her passion, in contrast to her earlier ice, burned through his body, incinerating his soul. Moments before, he'd felt dark and angry, rebuffed in all his efforts to show he cared, to make her birthday special, and to compensate for those three little words he could not say.

But now, as they desperately ripped off each other's clothes on his desk, as they kissed and suckled and licked, he felt her soft body move and sway beneath him, pulling him deeper, deeper. And suddenly those same unthinkable, forbidden three words rose in his heart, like sunlight bursting through a dark cloud.

Could he…? Did he…?

Bree moved, rolling him beneath her on the desk. Her silken thighs wrapped around his hips. He looked up at her expressive face, at her breasts swaying like music. A glowing sunset through the study's window washed her pale shoulders red, the color of a ruby.

The color of his heart.

With a gasp, she impaled herself upon him, pulling him deep inside her. As he filled her completely, for the first time in ten years everything was clear.

He loved her.

He'd been afraid to see it. He'd tried to deny it, to ignore it.

He'd buried himself in work, in sex, in dangerous sports. But he could not deny it any longer.

He loved her. The truth was he'd given her his heart long ago. When he thought she'd betrayed him, his heart had simply frozen, like an arctic sea. But from the moment he'd seen her again, across the poker table at the Hale Ka'nani, his heart had begun to thaw. Feeling the sting of her cold rejection today had taught him that he still felt pain. He still had a beating heart.

A heart that loved her.

Whatever the cost. Whatever the risk.

His love for her was absolute. He could not change it.

He wanted to go back in time and be the generous, trusting man he'd once been. He wanted to be the man who deserved Breanna Dalton.

When she gasped with pleasure, he tilted back his head and the first hoarse cry escaped his throat. Their joy built together, until he could no longer tell where his voice ended and hers began.

With a final cry, she collapsed in his arms. He held her tightly, both of them still sprawled on his desk. As he stroked her naked back, his heart pounded in his chest. He wanted to blurt out the words. But words were cheap. He would show her, the only way he knew how. He would do what terrified him most.

"I'm letting you go, Breanna," he said quietly. "I'm setting you free."

For a moment, he thought she hadn't heard. Then she lifted her head to look into his eyes. He'd thought she would be happy. Instead, she looked stricken, almost gutted.

Vladimir frowned.

"Don't you understand?" Reaching up, he caressed her cheek, tucking wild tendrils of sweaty blond hair behind her ear. "You're no longer my property. You're free."

"Why?" she choked out. "Why now?"

He smiled despite the lump in his throat. "Because…" Cupping her face with both his hands, he looked straight into her eyes. "I'm in love with you, Breanna."

Pulling back, she gasped, as if his words had caused her mortal injury.

He sat up on the desk beside her. "It took me ten years to realize what I should have admitted to myself long ago. I never stopped loving you. And I never will."

Blinking fast, she looked away.

"But what if I don't deserve your love?" she whispered. "What if I've done things that…"

"It doesn't matter." Gently, he turned her to face him. "Somehow, in spite of all my flaws, you decided to love me. I was too much of a coward to do the same." Lifting her hand to his lips, he kissed her skin fervently, then looked at her with tears in his eyes. "Until now."

She sucked in her breath.

"Whatever you do," he said quietly, searching her gaze, "for the rest of your life, I will love you. For the rest of mine."

Bree started to speak, then shook her head as silent tears spilled down her cheeks.

Was she so amazed, then, that he could return her love? The thought of that shamed him, reminding him how selfish he'd been. Pulling her back into his arms, he held her. When she claimed she was too tired to eat dinner, he took her to bed. He held her through the night as she cried herself to sleep. He didn't understand her tears. But as Vladimir stroked her hair and naked back, he vowed that he would never give her any reason to cry again. Ever.

His heart was irrevocably hers. But she was free.

Would she choose to stay with him? Or would she go?

Shortly before midnight, when Breanna finally slept, Vladimir realized he had to prepare for the worst. Pulling on a robe, he quietly left their bedroom and went downstairs to his office. Turning on his computer by habit, he looked for his cell phone. He'd order the jet to be available in the morning, to take her wherever she wanted to go. Then he prayed he could convince her to stay....

His foot slid on the mess of papers scattered across the floor. In the dim glow of light from the computer screen, the first words on the page of a contract he'd never noticed before caught his eye. Bending over, he picked it up.

I hereby renounce all shares in Xendzov Mining OAO...

His heart stopped in his chest. Hand shaking, he turned on a lamp, thrusting the paper beneath the light.

...giving them freely and in perpetuity to my brother, Kasimir.

He read it again. Then again.

This contract had been slyly slipped into the pile of papers on his desk. And with sickening certainty Vladimir knew how it had gotten there. Only one person could have done it.

He closed his eyes. When he'd first seen Bree in Hawaii, he'd assumed she was there to con someone. Later he'd convinced himself that meeting her at that poker game had been wild, pure coincidence. Even when he'd discovered from Greg Hudson that Kasimir had deliberately tried to plot that meeting, he'd convinced himself that Breanna, at least, was innocent.

Exhaling, he crushed the paper against his chest.

But his first instincts had been right all along. She'd been in Honolulu for a con. And just like ten years ago, Vladimir had been her mark.

As he opened his eyes, the dark shadows of his study were bleak. All color had been drained from the world, leaving only gray.

Bree and his brother had to be working together. After Vladimir had started attending private poker games in Honolulu, while recuperating from his racing accident, Kasimir had arranged for Bree to get a job there. His brother must have known all along that she was the poison Vladimir could not resist. The poker game, the wager, the whole affair had been a setup from start to finish.

All so that Bree could infiltrate his house and infiltrate his soul.

All so that Vladimir would sign this document.

His hands shook as he looked down at the contract.

His brother had baited his hook well. And so had she.

Bree had tricked him, the same way she'd done ten years ago. And Vladimir was so stupid that instead of being on his guard, he'd been fooled even worse than before. He thought of how he'd tried to please her, giving her his great-grandmother's peridot, buying her a puppy, buying her a hotel, and worst of all, declaring his love—when all the time, all he was to her…was a job.

He leaned back wearily in his desk chair. Just hours before, the purpose and meaning of his life had seemed so clear. So bright and full of promise. He'd felt young again, young and fearless. For that one shining moment, he'd been exactly the man he'd always wanted to be.

Rising to his feet, Vladimir poured himself a glass of vodka over ice. Going to the window, he swirled the tumbler, watching the prisms of the ice gleam in the scattered moonlight.

He could still destroy her.

Destroy Breanna? The thought made him choke out a low sob and claw back his hair.

Was there any way he could be wrong? Any way she could be innocent?

All the evidence pointed against her. It was obvious she was guilty. He looked down at the contract on his desk.

But should he believe the proof of his eyes?

Or the proof of his heart?

Standing alone in the shadows of his study, Vladimir drank the vodka in one gulp and put the glass down softly on a table.

Loving her had brought him to life again. Going back to the window, he opened it and leaned against the sill. He took a deep breath of the cold air, smelling the frozen sea, hearing the plaintive cry of distant, unseen birds. Midnight in Russia, in January, was frozen and white, gray and dead.

But still, he knew spring would come.

He took another deep breath. Everything had changed for him. And yet nothing had.

He loved her. And he always would.

Vladimir looked back down at the unsigned contract. In a sudden movement, he leaned over the polished wood of his desk where, hours ago, he'd made love to her, the woman he loved. Where he'd looked into her beautiful face and told her his love for her would last forever.

Slowly he reached for an expensive ballpoint pen. He looked down, reading for the tenth time the contract that would forever give his billion-dollar company to his brother.

And then, with a jagged scrawl, Vladimir signed his name.

The warm sunlight on Bree's face woke her from a vivid dream. She'd been standing with Vladimir on a beach in Hawaii, the surf rushing against their bare feet, the warm wind filled with the scent of flowers as they spoke their wedding vows.

Vladimir's eyes looked blue as the sea. *I, Vladimir, take you, Breanna, to be my wife....*

Smiling to herself, still drowsing, Bree reached out her arm. But his side of the bed was empty.

With a gasp, she sat up.

Last night, she'd thrown herself at Vladimir because she'd been physically unable to let him sign away his company to his brother. But she still didn't know what to do. She couldn't betray him. Or her sister.

I'm in love with you, Breanna. I never stopped loving you. And I never will.

She trembled, blinking back tears.

He loved her.

But even before he'd spoken the words, she should have known. He'd shown her his love a hundred times over, with each gift more precious than the last. Bree looked down at Snowy, curled up in a ball at the foot of her bed. Vladimir dreamed bigger things for her than she dared dream for herself, buying her a Hawaiian resort to support her dream of running a small bed-and-breakfast. And last night, he'd set her free. He'd sacrificed his own needs for hers.

Bree took a deep breath, setting her jaw.

She was going to tell him everything.

Pulling on a T-shirt and jeans, she went downstairs, her whole body shaking with fear. She tried not to think of Josie, or the risk she was taking. When Bree told him her sister was in danger, he wouldn't coldly reply that Josie should face the consequences of her own actions. Would he? He would help Bree save her.

But if he didn't…

Oh, God. She couldn't even think of it.

Going down the hallway, she looked in his office. It was empty. Her cheeks grew hot as she saw the desk where they'd made love so passionately last night. Then she stiffened. With an intake of breath, she rushed into the room and rifled quickly through the documents now stacked neatly on his desk, intending to destroy the contract before Vladimir ever saw it.

Then she gasped. Lifting the page, she stared at his scrawled signature.

He'd done it.

He must have had no idea what he was signing. But he'd transferred his company to his younger brother.

Bree closed her eyes, holding the paper to her chest. Why had he finally decided to love her now, of all times? It had taken Vladimir ten years to trust her again. It would take a single act for her to wipe that trust off the earth forever.

But what if this was a sign? What if this was the universe telling her what to do?

Midnight tonight was the deadline to save her sister, and Bree held in her hands the golden ticket. And unlike Vladimir's mercy, it was guaranteed. She could exchange it for Josie, then return to Russia and beg for Vladimir's forgiveness. After all, if anyone was going to be thrown on his mercy, shouldn't it be Bree herself, not her helpless younger sister?

Even if I give Kasimir this contract, it'll never stand in any court, she told herself. Vladimir was powerful, well connected. He would be fine.

Even if he had enemies aplenty who would rejoice to see his downfall....

I'm in love with you, Breanna. She whimpered as she remembered the dark midnight of Vladimir's eyes, the hoarse rasp of his voice. *I never stopped loving you.*

With a choked sob, she ran upstairs. Not letting herself look at the mussed-up sheets of the bed where he'd held her last night as she wept, she packed up her duffel bag, tucking the paper beneath her passport.

"Are you leaving?"

Looking up with an intake of breath, she saw Vladimir in the doorway, wearing a black button-down shirt and black trousers. His face was half-hidden in the shadow.

She swallowed. "Yes." She turned away. "You set me free. So I'm going." *Forgive me. I can't take the chance.*

He exhaled, and came closer. When she clearly saw his face, she nearly staggered back, shocked at the luminous pain in his eyes. Then she blinked, and it was gone.

"I have a plane waiting to take you wherever you want to go," he said.

"Just like that?"

"Just like that."

"You knew I would leave?"

"Yes." Lifting his gaze to hers, he whispered, "But I hoped you wouldn't. I hoped you could—love me—enough."

Her heart was slamming against her chest. She wanted to sob, to throw her arms around him, to pull out the contract and rip it up in front of his eyes. "Perhaps I'll come back."

"Perhaps," he said, but his lips twisted. "And Snowy? Are you leaving her behind?"

"Of course not," Bree said, shocked. "I wouldn't abandon her!"

"No," he replied quietly. "I know that. You wouldn't abandon anyone you truly loved."

Bree swallowed. "Vladimir, I told you the truth. I do love you. But I—"

"You don't have to explain." His eyes met hers. "Just be happy, Bree. That's all I want. All I've ever wanted."

"Your great-grandmother's necklace is on the nightstand," she said in a small voice.

"That was a gift." Picking up the necklace, he held it out to her. "Take it."

She shook her head. "That belongs to…to your future wife."

Coming up behind her, he said softly, "It belongs to you."

He put the necklace around her neck. She felt the cool, hard stone against her skin, and grief crashed over her like a wave. Closing her eyes, she sagged back against him. He wrapped his arms around her, cradling her against his chest for a single moment.

Then he let her go.

"I will always love you, Breanna," he said in a low voice. He turned away. "Goodbye."

Vladimir left their bedroom without looking back. She wanted to chase after him. She wanted to fall at his knees, weeping and begging for his forgiveness.

But she couldn't. She had the signed contract. Fate had made the decision for her.

It won't stand up in court, she told herself again, her teeth chattering. *After Josie's safe, I'll come back. I will somehow make him forgive me….*

Bree had no memory of collecting Snowy and her duffel bag. But somehow, twenty minutes later, they were in the back of the limo, driving away from the palace. Her puppy sat in her lap, whining as she looked through the window at Vladimir's palace, then plaintively up at her mistress.

As Bree looked back at the fairy-tale palace, snow sparkled on Vladimir's wide fields and on the forest of bare, black trees around the palace of blue and gold. And she realized she was weeping, pressing her hand against the necklace at her throat.

Bree felt something prick her finger. Looking down, she saw the peridot's sharp edge had pricked her skin. A Russian prince had once sent his beloved wife and child into the safety of exile, with this necklace as their only memento of him, before he'd died alone in Siberia, in ultimate sacrifice.

A sob rose to Bree's lips. As Vladimir had sacrificed…

Her eyes widened. With an intake of breath, she looked back at the palace.

You knew I would leave?

Yes. His eyes had seared hers, straight through her soul. *But I hoped you wouldn't. I hoped you could—love me—enough.*

What had Vladimir sacrificed for her?

Was it possible…that he *knew?*

"Stop," she cried to the driver. "Turn around! Go back!"

The puppy barked madly, turning circles in her lap as the limo stopped, struggling to turn around on the long, slender road surrounded by snow.

Bree didn't care if the signed contract had miraculously fallen into her lap. She didn't care what the universe might be trying to tell her. *The choice was still hers.*

All this time, she'd thought she had to choose between the two people she loved. She didn't.

She just had to choose herself.

Ten years ago, loving Vladimir had changed her. He'd given her a second chance at life. He'd shown her she could be something besides a poker-playing con artist with a flexible conscience. He'd made her want to be *more.* To be honest and true, not just when it was convenient, but always.

This was the woman she was born to be.

And she would never be anything else ever again. Not for any price.

Before the limo stopped in the courtyard, Bree had thrown open the door, leaving her duffel bag and valuables behind as she leaped headlong into the snow. Her puppy bounded beside her, barking frantically as Bree ran straight back to the only answer her heart had ever wanted.

She found him in his study, standing by the window that overlooked the sea.

"Vladimir," she cried.

Slowly he turned, his handsome face like granite. It was only when she came closer that she saw the tears sparkling in his eyes.

He wasn't made of ice. He was flesh and blood. And letting her go had ripped him to the bone.

Choking back a sob, she threw herself into his arms. She jumped up, hugging him even with her legs. Startled, he caught her, holding her against him.

"Are you really here?" he breathed, stroking her hair, as if he thought she was a dream. "You were free. You had the signed contract. Why did you return?"

Bree slowly slid down his body, her eyes wide. "You knew."

Blinking fast, Vladimir nodded.

"Why did you do it?" she said. "Why would you set me free, when you knew you'd lose everything?"

His phone rang from his pocket, but he ignored it. He cupped her face, tracing his thumbs against her trembling mouth. "Because I knew I'd already lost everything, if you walked out my door." He shook his head. "I had to know. If you really loved me. Or if you…didn't."

"And what did you decide?" she whispered through numb lips.

"I decided it didn't matter." He looked straight into her eyes. "I meant what I said. Whatever you do, I will love you, Breanna. For the rest of my life."

She burst into tears, pressing her face against his chest. "I'm sorry," she sobbed as her tears soaked his shirt. "I was wrong to think I could ever betray you."

He stroked her hair gently. "Did my brother promise you money to pay off your old debts? Is that why you agreed to help him?"

"*Help* him?" Drawing back, Bree looked at Vladimir. "I had no idea he was behind us getting jobs in Hawaii. Not until he threatened me!"

Vladimir's hand grew still. "He threatened you?"

"At the New Year's Eve ball."

He sucked in his breath. "Kasimir was there?"

"He found me on the dance floor when I was alone. Right after I told you I loved you—when you took off...."

"*That* was why you've been acting so distant?" Vladimir looked at her, his expression fierce. "What did he say to you?"

A lump rose in her throat.

"He's married Josie," she whispered. "He's holding her hostage."

"What?" Vladimir cried.

"He wanted to get back your family's land, and it was the only way to break the trust. Josie agreed to marry him, because she thought it was the only way to save me."

"From what?" he demanded.

"From you." With a bitter laugh, Bree wiped her eyes. "Funny, isn't it?"

His face filled with cold rage. His phone started ringing again. He didn't move a muscle to answer. "Hilarious."

"He said if I ever wanted to see her again, I had to bring the signed contract to his house in Marrakech before midnight tonight."

Vladimir looked ready to commit murder. "Why didn't you tell me?"

"I'm sorry," Bree said miserably. "I was afraid you'd say it was Josie's own fault, and that she should face the consequences."

He scowled. "She's just a kid. I never meant she should—" He broke off with a curse as, for the third time in five minutes, his phone started ringing again. He snatched it up angrily. "What the hell do you want?"

Then Vladimir froze.

"Kasimir," he said quietly. "About time."

Stricken, Bree held her breath, staring up at him.

His eyes narrowed. "She already told me. Your plan to turn us against each other didn't work." He listened, then paced three steps. "I am willing to make the trade."

Bree covered her mouth with her hands, realizing that Vladimir was offering to give up his billion-dollar company to save her baby sister. Then he scowled.

"Kasimir, don't be a fool! You can still—"

Vladimir stopped, then pulled the phone from his ear, staring at it in shock.

"What happened?" Bree said anxiously. "What did he say? Is he willing to make the trade?"

"No," Vladimir said, sounding dazed. "He said he no longer has any intention of divorcing her. He told me I could keep my stupid company."

Her mouth dropped open. "He said that?"

"His exact words." Vladimir's lips twisted. "It seems he cares about keeping her more than hurting me."

Bree took a deep breath. She could still hear Kasimir's cold words. *What I want is revenge. And I will have it.* "I'm not so sure…."

Then she remembered the anger in his blue eyes.

So much for Josie's sacrifice, he'd accused her bitterly.

Bree had wondered about that then. It seemed even more certain now. She licked her lips. "Is it possible…he *could* care for her?"

"I don't know about that. But he won't hurt her. My brother had—has—a good heart."

"How can you say that, after how he's tried to destroy you?"

Vladimir's jaw tightened.

"Perhaps he had a good cause," he admitted in a low voice. Shaking his head, he continued, "But your sister is in no danger. Kasimir hates me, and perhaps you. But he has no quarrel with her."

"If I could only be absolutely sure—"

"She is safe," Vladimir said simply. "I would stake my life on it. And the fact that he actually wants to stay married to her..." He slowly smiled. "It's interesting. Very interesting."

His phone rang abruptly in his hand, and he put it to his ear. "Hello?"

Kasimir? Bree mouthed.

He shook his head at her, his hand tightening on the phone. "Lefèvre, at last. Give me some good news." He listened. And then a smile lifted his handsome face. Seeing that smile, Bree's heart soared. She suddenly knew everything was going to be all right.

He hung up. "My investigator has found her."

Bree gave a joyful sob. "Where is she?"

"Safe." His smile widened. "And very close."

Bree started to turn. "We should go to her—"

Vladimir grabbed her by the wrist. "First things first," he growled. "I want to do this before anything else comes between us." And before her amazed eyes, he fell to one knee.

"I don't have a ring," he said quietly, "because I didn't let myself hope this could happen." Quirking a dark eyebrow, he gave her a cheeky grin. "And I think I'd better let you pick out your own ring, in any case."

She held her breath.

His darkly handsome face grew serious. Vulnerable.

"Will you marry me?" he whispered.

Marry him? Bree's heart galloped. Vladimir wanted her to be his wife, the mother of his children—just like she'd dreamed?

He swallowed, and his stark blue eyes became uncertain.

"Will you have me, Breanna?" Reaching up, he gripped her hands in his own. "Will you be mine?"

Tears rose to her eyes.

"I am yours already. Don't you remember?" The corners of her trembling lips tugged upwards. "You own me, heart and soul."

He exhaled in a rush. "Does that mean you'll be my wife?"

"Yes." Tears streamed unchecked down her cheeks as she pulled on his hands, lifting him to his feet. "With all my heart."

Vladimir cupped her cheek. "I belong to you," he vowed. "Now and forever."

As their white Russian puppy leaped and barked in happy circles around their feet, he wrapped Bree in his arms. Lowering his head, he kissed her with the passion and adoration that promised a lifetime. And she knew, come what may, that he would always love her, because she'd been brave enough to love herself.

"Never play with your heart, kiddo," her father had once told her. "Only a sucker plays with his heart. Even if you win, you lose."

But as Bree looked up into the face of the man she loved, the man she would soon wed, the man who would bring Josie safely home—she suddenly knew her father was wrong. Because when the chips were down, love was the only thing worth a risk. The only thing worth gambling for.

Playing with all your heart...was the *only* way to win.

* * * * *

COMING NEXT MONTH from Harlequin Presents®
AVAILABLE FEBRUARY 19, 2013

#3121 PLAYING THE DUTIFUL WIFE
Carol Marinelli

When Meg Hamilton learns that her estranged husband, Niklas Dos Santos, needs her help she agrees, but only in exchange for his signature on the divorce papers. Except she hadn't bargained on their mind-blowing connection being as undeniable as ever.

#3122 A SCANDAL, A SECRET, A BABY
Sharon Kendrick

Wickedly sexy—and impossibly ruthless— Dante D'Arezzo is the last person Justina wants to see. He broke her heart once; she won't surrender to his insatiable desire again. But what Dante wants, he gets—no matter the consequences!

#3123 THE FALLEN GREEK BRIDE
The Disgraced Copelands
Jane Porter

Infamous Morgan Copeland's reputation is in tatters. Holding on to the last shreds of her pride, she must seek help from the most merciless man she knows... her husband, Drakon Xanthis. Her only bargaining chip? Her body!

#3124 A REPUTATION FOR REVENGE
Princes Untamed
Jennie Lucas

Revenge is at Kasimir's fingertips; the champagne is on ice and his new wife, Josie, waits in the bedroom— and victory has never tasted sweeter. But Josie's purity tests the one thing Kasimir didn't know he had—*honor.*

You can find more information on upcoming Harlequin® titles, free excerpts and more at www.Harlequin.com.

HPCNM0213RAR

#3125 THE NOTORIOUS GABRIEL DIAZ
Cathy Williams

The last time Gabriel Diaz heard the word *no* was when Lucy Robins rejected his skilled advances. Now she stands before him offering a deal—but just how high a price will Gabriel expect, and is Lucy ready to pay it?

#3126 TAMING THE LAST ACOSTA
Susan Stephens

Living her life vicariously through her camera, photojournalist Romy Winner is happy to stay in the background.... Until former Argentinian polo champion turned Special Forces soldier Kruz Acosta challenges her to step out of the shadows—and into his bed!

#3127 CAPTIVE IN THE SPOTLIGHT
Annie West

Domenico Volpe's life has been paparazzi fodder for years...glitz, glamour and lastly a family tragedy. He's determined to keep Lucy Knight—the woman at the center of it all—quiet, even if that means locking her away with him on his island!

#3128 ISLAND OF SECRETS
Robyn Donald

Luc MacAllister believes Joanna Forman is a gold digger of the worst kind, but they need each other if they are to get their hands on their inheritance. Yet the sizzling attraction that burns between them threatens to ruin it all....

You can find more information on upcoming Harlequin® titles, free excerpts and more at www.Harlequin.com.

HPCNM0213RB

REQUEST YOUR FREE BOOKS!

2 FREE NOVELS PLUS
2 FREE GIFTS!

YES! Please send me 2 FREE Harlequin Presents® novels and my 2 FREE gifts (gifts are worth about $10). After receiving them, if I don't wish to receive any more books, I can return the shipping statement marked "cancel." If I don't cancel, I will receive 6 brand-new novels every month and be billed just $4.30 per book in the U.S. or $4.99 per book in Canada. That's a saving of at least 14% off the cover price! It's quite a bargain! Shipping and handling is just 50¢ per book in the U.S. and 75¢ per book in Canada.* I understand that accepting the 2 free books and gifts places me under no obligation to buy anything. I can always return a shipment and cancel at any time. Even if I never buy another book, the two free books and gifts are mine to keep forever.

106/306 HDN FVRK

Name	(PLEASE PRINT)
Address	Apt. #
City	State/Prov. Zip/Postal Code

Signature (if under 18, a parent or guardian must sign)

Mail to the **Harlequin® Reader Service:**
IN U.S.A.: P.O. Box 1867, Buffalo, NY 14240-1867
IN CANADA: P.O. Box 609, Fort Erie, Ontario L2A 5X3

Are you a current subscriber to Harlequin Presents books and want to receive the larger-print edition?
Call 1-800-873-8635 or visit www.ReaderService.com.

* Terms and prices subject to change without notice. Prices do not include applicable taxes. Sales tax applicable in N.Y. Canadian residents will be charged applicable taxes. Offer not valid in Quebec. This offer is limited to one order per household. Not valid for current subscribers to Harlequin Presents books. All orders subject to credit approval. Credit or debit balances in a customer's account(s) may be offset by any other outstanding balance owed by or to the customer. Please allow 4 to 6 weeks for delivery. Offer available while quantities last.

Your Privacy—The Harlequin® Reader Service is committed to protecting your privacy. Our Privacy Policy is available online at www.ReaderService.com or upon request from the Harlequin Reader Service.

We make a portion of our mailing list available to reputable third parties that offer products we believe may interest you. If you prefer that we not exchange your name with third parties, or if you wish to clarify or modify your communication preferences, please visit us at www.ReaderService.com/consumerchoice or write to us at Harlequin Reader Service Preference Service, P.O. Box 9062, Buffalo, NY 14269. Include your complete name and address.

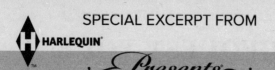
*Josie Dalton will do anything to get her sister back,
even if it means marrying a prince whose reputation
is world-renowned!*

Read on for a sneak preview of
A REPUTATION FOR REVENGE
from USA TODAY *bestselling author Jennie Lucas.*

* * *

"You're an unusual girl, Josie Dalton."

Unusual didn't sound good. "I am?" she echoed uncertainly, lowering the glass.

"It's refreshing to be with a woman who makes absolutely no effort to impress me."

She snorted. "Trying to impress you would be a waste of time. A man like you would never be interested in a girl like me—not *genuinely* interested," she mumbled.

Kasimir looked down at her, his blue eyes breathtaking.

"You're selling yourself short," he said softly, and Josie felt it again—that strange flash of heat.

She swallowed. "You're being nice, but I know there's no point in pretending to be something I'm not."

"Unusual. And honest." Turning, he went to the wet bar and poured himself a short glass of amber-colored liquid. He returned, then took a slow, thoughtful sip.

"All right. I'll get your sister back for you," he said abruptly.

"You will!" If there was something strange about his tone, Josie was too weak with relief to notice. "When?"

"After we're wed. Our marriage will last until the land in Alaska is legally transferred to me." He looked straight into her eyes. "And I'll bring her to you, and set you both free. Is that what you want?"

Isn't that what she'd just said? "Yes," she cried.

Setting down his drink on the polished wooden table, he held out his hand. "Deal."

Slowly she reached out her hand. She felt the hot, calloused hollow of his palm, felt his strong fingers interlace with hers. A tremble raced through her. Swallowing, she lifted her gaze to his handsome face, to those electric blue eyes, and it was like staring straight at the sun.

"I h-hope it won't be too painful for you," she stammered, "being married to me."

His hand tightened over hers.

"As you'll be my only wife, ever," he said softly, "I think I'll enjoy you a great deal."

* * *

Discover A REPUTATION FOR REVENGE
February 19, 2013, from Harlequin Presents®!

Copyright © 2013 by Jennifer Ness

HPEXP0213-1

SPECIAL EXCERPT FROM

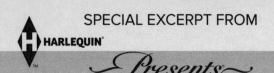

HARLEQUIN®

~Presents~

Life for the Copeland family was filled with unrivaled luxury—until scandalous allegations rocked their foundations, forcing Morgan Copeland to turn to the one man she never wanted to see again. Her husband!

Read on for an exciting excerpt from the first book in a fantastic new miniseries, THE DISGRACED COPELANDS, by sensational author Jane Porter!

* * *

HE was going to kiss her. And she wanted the kiss, craved his kiss, even as a little voice of reason inside her head sounded the alarm….

Stop. Wait. Think.

Morgan had to remember…remember the past…remember what had happened last time…. This wasn't just a kiss, but an inferno. If she gave in, it would be all over. Drakon was so dangerous for her. He did something to her. He, like his name, Drakon, Greek for dragon, was powerful, potent and destructive.

But he was also beautiful, physical and sensual. He made her feel. My God, he made her *feel,* and she wanted that intensity now.

"My beautiful, expensive mistake," he murmured, his lips brushing across the shell of her ear, making her breath catch in her throat and sending hot darts of delicious sensation throughout her body.

"Next time, don't marry the girl," she said, trying to sound brazen and cavalier but failing miserably.

"Would you have been happier as my mistress?" he asked, his tongue tracing the curve of her ear even as his muscular thigh pressed up, his knee against her core, teasing her senses, making her shiver with need. "Would you have been able to let go more? Enjoyed the sex without guilt?" he added, biting her tender earlobe, his teeth sharp, even as he wedged his thigh deeper between her knees.

"There was no guilt," she choked, eyes closing as he worked his thigh against her in a slow maddening circle. She knew it was wrong, but she wanted more, not less.

"Liar." He leaned in closer, his hips pressing down against her hips, making her feel hot. "You liked it hot. You liked it when I made you fall apart."

And it was true, she thought, her body so tight and hot and aching that she arched against him, absolutely wanton. There was no satisfaction like this, though, and she wanted satisfaction. Wanted him. Wanted him here and now.

* * *

*Find out what price Drakon puts on Morgan's redemption in THE FALLEN GREEK BRIDE,
available February 19, 2013, from Harlequin Presents®!*

Copyright © 2013 by Jane Porter

HPEXP0213-2

HARLEQUIN *Presents*

Glamorous international settings...
powerful men...passionate romances.

**Enjoy twice the scandal and seduction
next month!**

Look for an extra reader-favorite story included
in each **March 2013** Harlequin Presents® book!

2 GREAT
NOVELS
SAME GREAT
PRICE

Collect all 8 books and enjoy even more of the
brooding billionaires, untamed princes and
sensual romances you love!

Available wherever books are sold.

www.Harlequin.com

HPVA0213